RUNAWAY

Jessica heard the phone clattering down and the boy yelling for Nicky in the background. After a couple of minutes, the phone was picked up again.

"Yeah?" It was Nicky's voice.

"Hi, it's Jessica." Just the sound of his voice made her feel better, convinced her that she was doing the right thing.

"Hi," he said softly. "I was just going to call you."

"You were?"

"Yeah. Listen, I'm leaving tonight."

"Tonight?" Jessica panicked. "I thought you weren't going until Friday!"

"Things have gotten really bad around here after last night. I've got to get out now."

Jessica didn't know how to reply.

After a short silence, Nicky spoke again. "Have you been thinking about my offer?"

Jessica took a deep breath. "Actually, that's what I called to talk to you about."

Bantam Books in the Sweet Valley High Series
Ask your bookseller for the books you have missed

SWEET VALLEY HIGH

RUNAWAY

Written by
Kate William

Created by
FRANCINE PASCAL

BANTAM BOOKS
TORONTO • NEW YORK • LONDON • SYDNEY • AUCKLAND

RL 5, IL age 12 and up

RUNAWAY
A Bantam Book / December 1986

Sweet Valley High is a trademark of Francine Pascal

Conceived by Francine Pascal

Produced by Cloverdale Press, Inc.

Cover art by James Mathewuse

ISBN 0-553-26682-9

Published simultaneously in the United States and Canada

Bantam Books are published by Bantam Books, Inc. Its trademark, consisting of the words "Bantam Books" and the portrayal of a rooster, is Registered in U.S. Patent and Trademark Office and in other countries. Marca Registrada. Bantam Books, Inc., 666 Fifth Avenue, New York, New York 10103.

PRINTED IN THE UNITED STATES OF AMERICA

O   15   14   13   12   11   10   9   8   7

To Jeanne Rubin

One

Elizabeth searched through her closet one more time without success. It was no use; her new blue silk blouse wasn't there.

Elizabeth stomped angrily through the bathroom that connected her bedroom to Jessica's, her twin sister, and burst into the room without knocking. Jessica was lying on her stomach on her unmade bed, her long, tan legs hanging off the edge. She was leafing through the pages of a magazine.

As usual Jessica's room was in a state of disarray. Every surface was strewn with clothes, magazines, and makeup. To Elizabeth it looked a little like the aftermath of a bargain-basement sale at a department store.

Elizabeth cleared her throat. Jessica didn't even look up.

"Jessica!" Elizabeth said as forcefully as she could.

"Uh-huh?"

Elizabeth crossed her arms and tapped her foot on the floor. "I can't seem to find my new blue blouse that I have not even worn once. I thought you might know something about it."

Jessica still didn't look up from the magazine. "Uh-huh," she repeated.

Elizabeth stepped over to the bed and snatched the magazine out of her twin's hands.

"Hey," Jessica said, looking up in surprise.

"I'm talking to you, Jess."

Jessica smiled innocently at her twin, her blue-green eyes wide and a sweet smile on her lips. "What was it, Liz?"

"I am looking for my blue silk blouse, which has mysteriously disappeared from my closet. Now, I doubt very much that it walked away all by itself."

"Oh, that," Jessica said calmly. She went to her closet and pulled out the blouse. "Here, Liz. I'm sorry. I know I should have asked you, but I needed it in a hurry. I had a date with Neil, and he's seen everything in my closet at least a hundred and thirty-seven times."

Elizabeth shook her head. She doubted that her twin had worn very much of her wardrobe twice, let alone a hundred thirty-seven times.

Jessica handed Elizabeth the blouse and returned

to the bed. "The problem is, Liz, you're never around here when any of us needs you. You're always off with Todd or working on something for the newspaper. You really have to try to understand that your first allegiance should be to your family, those who love you best."

Elizabeth couldn't believe her ears. Jessica was in rare form that day. After borrowing her blouse without permission, she was now trying to turn Elizabeth's anger into guilt. It was true that Elizabeth spent a lot of time with her boyfriend, Todd Wilkins, and she was a dedicated reporter for *The Oracle*, Sweet Valley High's newspaper, but that didn't give Jessica the right to grab anything she wanted from Elizabeth's closet.

"Jessica . . ." Elizabeth began.

Her twin cut her off. "It's all right, Liz. I forgive you."

Elizabeth stared at her twin, not sure whether to laugh or to scream.

"It's funny," Jessica went on, not missing a beat. "I thought I heard Steve's voice a minute ago."

At the mention of her brother, Elizabeth's anger disappeared. She had planned on telling her twin about Steven, but she had gotten sidetracked when she started looking for her blouse.

"You did hear Steve, Jess," Elizabeth said solemnly, sitting down on the bed.

"Why? I thought his term break wasn't for a couple of weeks."

"It isn't. He left school."

Elizabeth watched as the realization of what she had said crept across her twin's face.

Jessica gasped. "He quit?"

Elizabeth sat down on the bed and began to play with a corner of the blanket. "Yes. Just for the rest of the term."

"It's because of Tricia, isn't it?" Jessica asked.

Elizabeth nodded. "He's just having a real hard time dealing with the whole thing. He thought it might be better if he took some time off from school to pull himself together."

Steven Wakefield had loved Tricia Martin deeply. They'd managed to stay together in spite of differences in their backgrounds, problems with Tricia's self-image, even Jessica's well-intentioned tampering. In the end, the only thing that could separate them was the leukemia that had taken Tricia's life a few months earlier.

Steven had been shattered by the loss of the only girl he had ever really loved. Tricia's death had been a terribly difficult experience for him, and the passage of time had only seemed to increase his pain and loneliness.

The twins had noticed their brother pulling away ever since the funeral. When he'd come home on weekends he'd seemed more and more distant.

Now, Steven was only a shadow of his former self. He didn't go out, he didn't laugh much, and he hardly ever saw his friends.

"He really looks terrible," Elizabeth went on. "He just came in and said he was taking some time away from school."

"What did Mom and Dad say?"

"Well, they weren't exactly thrilled, but they didn't pressure him about it. I just feel so bad for him, Jess. I mean, I can't help thinking about how I'd feel if something terrible happened to Todd. I'd probably be the same way. I just can't imagine what it must feel like to lose someone you love that much."

Jessica felt a momentary twinge of guilt as she remembered how poorly she had spoken of Tricia when she was alive. She had never thought Tricia was a good match for Steven, mostly because of Tricia's family. Her father was an alcoholic and her sister Betsy had had a bad reputation. Jessica had even tried to get Steven away from Tricia and to fix him up with Cara Walker, her best friend, but Steven wasn't interested.

Jessica got up and walked over to her dresser. She reached under a pile of scarves and sweaters and extracted her hairbrush. It was amazing to Elizabeth how Jessica could find anything in that mess, but her twin seemed to have her own sense of order. For Jessica, it was perfectly natural to keep her hairbrush under six sweaters and nine scarves.

Jessica walked back to the bed and plopped down next to Elizabeth. She began pulling the brush through her shoulder-length blond hair. "Look, Liz," she said coldly, "I am as sorry as anyone about Tricia. I know Steve was devoted to her, and I feel bad about the whole thing, too, but he has just got to get over it and join the world of the living."

"I know," Elizabeth said. "But I don't think he's going to do it all by himself. It's just too hard."

Jessica smiled. "Are you suggesting that we help him along?"

"Well, nothing obvious, like inviting his friends over. It might make him uncomfortable." Elizabeth began to consider the possibilities. "It's so hard with school being out next week. There aren't any dances or games or anything."

"Cara's having a party tomorrow night," Jessica offered.

Elizabeth's face lit up at the idea. "That's not a bad idea. I'm sure there'll be lots of people there that Steve knows."

Jessica shook her head. "I don't know, Liz. You know how Steve feels about Cara."

"Oh, that's all in the past. I'm sure Steve likes Cara," Elizabeth countered.

"Yeah." Jessica laughed. "About as much as the flu."

"Anyway," Elizabeth went on, "it isn't like we're setting up a date or anything. It would just be an evening out."

"He won't go for it," Jessica said, shaking out her hair. "But if you think it's worth a try, go ahead and ask him."

"Actually," Elizabeth said tentatively, "I think it would be a better idea if you asked him."

"No way, Liz," Jessica said, her voice rising. "He's still mad at me for the last time I tried to get him and Cara together."

"Calm down, Jessica. I've got reasons."

Jessica walked to the dresser and stuffed the brush back under the piles of scarves and sweaters. "Yeah, so do I. Like I don't want to spend the rest of the year in traction."

"Listen." Elizabeth sat her sister back down on the bed. "First of all, Cara is your best friend. It would be more natural for you to invite him. And second, I'm going with Todd, but you don't have a date yet. Do you?"

Jessica stared coldly at Elizabeth. "Thanks for reminding me."

Elizabeth went on. "You could say you don't have a date and you don't want to go alone."

"Be serious, Liz."

Elizabeth smiled. She did have to admit that it

seemed a little farfetched that her twin couldn't get a date. Jessica could usually get any one of a hundred guys to go out with her at the snap of her fingers.

"Come on, Jess," Elizabeth pleaded. "It's worth a try."

Jessica remained silent.

"For Steve," Elizabeth added.

Jessica looked at her sister's plaintive expression. Of course, it would be a nice thing to do for Steven, she thought, provided he'd go for it. And it was always possible that something still might be fixed up between him and Cara, and that would be wonderful. They'd both have Jessica to thank. It could all work out perfectly. Jessica frowned for a second as she thought how demeaning it would be to show up at Cara's party with her brother as her date. *But,* she reassured herself, *sometimes you just have to make sacrifices.*

"OK," Jessica said finally. "I'll bring it up at dinner."

"Great!"

"But it's a very difficult assignment," Jessica said slyly. "And I think it's pretty important that I look my best." Jessica smiled and looked down at the blue silk blouse in Elizabeth's lap.

Elizabeth rolled her eyes and handed her sister the blouse. "Here," she snapped.

Jessica took the blouse and kissed her sister on

the cheek. "Thank you, Liz. It's beautiful. You know, you're really developing good taste. I must've taught you something."

Elizabeth laughed and headed for the door. "More than you know, dear sister," she called behind her. "More than you know."

Jessica walked into the Wakefields' spacious Spanish-tiled kitchen. Her father, wearing an apron over his shirt and tie, was standing at a counter and fussing over the salad. On anyone else, the apron might have been comic, but Ned Wakefield was the kind of man who looked good in almost anything. Just then he seemed to be giving the salad the same concentration and commitment he gave his successful legal practice.

"Well, hello, princess." Mr. Wakefield smiled at Jessica. "Kiss any frogs today?"

Jessica walked over and gave him a kiss on the cheek. "Nope. You're the first."

"That's good." He laughed. "Have you seen your brother?"

Jessica got the water glasses out of the cupboard. "Not yet. When did he get in?"

"About an hour ago. He's taking a swim."

Mr. Wakefield's solemn expression indicated to Jessica how concerned he was about Steven. Suddenly she felt uncomfortable about the party idea.

Maybe it wasn't such a good one. Jessica was about to discuss it with her dad when Steven walked in.

One glance at her brother showed Jessica that Elizabeth was right. He didn't look good. It wasn't anything physical, especially now, after he'd finished a hard swim. His dark hair was pushed back, and his muscular build was emphasized by the cut-off jeans and sweat shirt he was wearing. He flashed a quick smile at Jessica and said hello. That was when Jessica really noticed the difference. His eyes. There didn't seem to be any light in them. It was as if something inside had burned out.

"You know," their father said, laughing, "I have never been able to teach your mother how to do justice to a salad. That woman has a master's degree, and she still can't mix a decent dressing."

"My master's was in design," Alice Wakefield called from the door. "You'd be surprised how few salad courses we had to take."

She breezed into the kitchen and walked to the oven. After pulling the roast out, she walked over to Steven and gave him a hug.

"Have a nice swim?" she said.

"Yeah." He smiled.

"Table set, Jessica?" she asked.

"I just have to get the silverware." Jessica pulled a drawer open, took out five knives, forks, and teaspoons, and started for the dining room.

"We're almost ready here," her mother said. "As soon as your father finishes with that salad."

"A proper salad has to be prepared with the care of a fine work of art," he said lightly. He put one last cherry tomato on top, picked up the salad bowl, and stepped back from the counter. "There!" he said. "Now we're ready."

Dinner that night had a special feeling. The Wakefields were concerned about Steven and had gone out of their way to make his homecoming a little easier for him. All his favorite foods were on the table, and everyone smiled a great deal. In speaking they all tried desperately to skirt around any topic that might remind him of Tricia.

Mr. Wakefield watched his son pick at the food. He turned to his wife and smiled. "The roast is perfect."

Everyone nodded and complimented the food, except Steven, whose mind seemed to be somewhere else entirely.

"Would you like some more peas, Steve?" Mrs. Wakefield asked.

"No, thanks," Steven muttered. "I'm still working on all of this."

There was an uncomfortable silence at the table. Mrs. Wakefield pushed back a strand of her golden hair. When Alice Wakefield was around, it was easy to see where the twins had gotten their striking looks. With her blond hair, blue eyes, and slim figure, it was almost possible to mistake her for the twins' older sister. She cleared her throat now. "So, you two have a whole week off from school."

"Yes, thank heavens." Jessica would rather do almost anything than go to classes, and the week's vacation was a welcome gift.

Her father looked up, smiling. "Any big plans?"

Just then Jessica felt Elizabeth kick her under the table. But Jessica didn't need prompting. She knew an opening when she saw one. "Well," she began, "nothing special. Cara is having a party tomorrow night."

"Oh, that sounds like fun," her mother said, helping herself to more of the roast.

"It's not a big thing," Jessica continued. "Just a bunch of people from school."

She looked hopefully at Steven, who didn't respond. He didn't even seem to be listening. He just sat at his place, brooding and pushing food around his plate with a fork.

"Who're you going with?" Mr. Wakefield asked.

Jessica couldn't believe her good luck. The conversation couldn't have gone any more smoothly if she'd given her family a script.

"Well, I haven't really got a date. I sort of waited until the last minute and then got stuck."

Ned Wakefield began buttering a roll. "Well, I'm sure you'll have a good time anyway." He turned to his other daughter. "I assume you're going with Todd."

"Of course." Elizabeth eyed Jessica hopefully.

"I'm not really wild about going alone," Jessica said slowly. "I thought maybe you'd like to come along, Steve."

Steven was quiet for a second, and Jessica thought he was considering her offer. "You're not going to start all that stuff with Cara again, are you?" he asked finally.

Jessica felt her footing collapse beneath her. "No, I just thought—"

Steven cut her off angrily. "When are you going to learn, Jess? I thought I made it perfectly clear that I'm not interested in Cara Walker. Not now or ever!"

Jessica tried to protest. "I wasn't trying to fix up anything. I just thought—"

Steven broke in again, "Why can't you just stop trying to manipulate all of our lives?"

For a second it looked as though he was going to go on, but instead, he just threw his napkin down and stormed out of the room.

Everyone was quiet for a moment. Mr. Wakefield spoke first. "Really, Jess. Don't you think it's a little too soon for anything like that?"

"Yes, Jessica," her mother added. "I would think you'd be a little more sensitive. It hasn't been that long since Tricia . . ." Her voice trailed off.

"It wasn't Jess's fault," Elizabeth said, rushing to her sister's defense. "It was my idea. I just thought it was about time Steve got his thoughts off Tricia. He can't sit around and mope for the rest of his life. I'm the one who brought it up. We didn't mean for it to sound like we were fixing him up with someone. We just wanted to help."

"Oh," Mrs. Wakefield said. "Well, I'm sorry to have jumped on you, Jess."

"Sure," Jessica spat out. "Now that Elizabeth explains it all, it's OK, right? If it was Elizabeth's idea, it must have been a good one." Jessica stood up. "May I be excused? I promised Cara I'd pick her up at seven-thirty, and it must be almost that now."

"If you're finished, of course," Mr. Wakefield said.

Jessica folded her napkin and walked out of the room.

Well, this is nothing new, Jessica told herself. *I swear—sometimes they just look for chances to jump all over me. They never do that with Elizabeth.*

Jessica hurried upstairs, got her shoulder bag, then ran out of the house. The red Fiat convertible she shared with her twin was in the driveway. She got in, started the engine, and let the motor run for a moment.

Sometimes I don't feel I'm even a part of this family. Her thoughts were racing almost as fast as the engine of the tiny sports car. *All I was trying to do was help Steve out of his depression, and I got yelled at from all sides. It's just not fair.*

Jessica was so lost in her thoughts that she didn't see Elizabeth approach.

Elizabeth rapped on the car window, and the sound broke Jessica out of her reverie. She rolled down the window and stared coldly at her sister.

"I'm sorry, Jess. If I'd known everyone was going to be so critical . . ."

"Forget it." Jessica put the Fiat into reverse. "I should've expected it."

"Expected what? What are you talking about?"

"Come on, Liz. You know what I mean. It's been the same all our lives, hasn't it?"

Elizabeth was becoming flustered. "Jess, you've got to understand—"

"Oh, I understand, all right," Jessica interrupted. "Everyone was worried about Steve, and they were all nervous, right? But I have feelings too, Liz. Do you think I like being treated like that?"

"Treated like what?"

Jessica stared at her twin. What was the use of trying to explain how she felt? Elizabeth would never understand. For her, everything always seemed so easy. Everyone trusted her; they all listened whenever she said something.

I'm just tired of being the bad twin, Jessica thought. *Sometimes, I wish I'd never been born.*

A moment later Jessica got control of her feelings and looked at Elizabeth calmly. "Never mind, Liz. It isn't important. Go back inside."

She rolled the window back up and backed the car out of the driveway. Elizabeth stood watching after the Fiat for a moment, wondering what had gotten into her sister this time.

Two

essica walked up to the counter of the Dairi Burger nd ordered a Tab.

"And I'd like a double cheeseburger and fries— nd a Tab," Cara said.

John Doherty, one of the owners of the popular ast-food restaurant, grinned at the two girls. "It'll e a couple of minutes on those fries." He handed hem their sodas. "Why don't you two sit down, nd I'll have someone bring the rest of your order o you."

"Sure," Cara said, smiling. They paid for the ood and wound their way past the wooden tables o a booth.

They settled into the booth, and Cara took a sip f her soda. "OK, so what's up?"

Jessica began to play with the ring of moisture

her paper cup was leaving on the table. "What do you mean, what's up?"

"Come on, Jess," Cara said. "For the last hour a little neon sign over your head has been flashing, 'Depression . . . Depression.' " Cara made little pulsing motions with her hands.

Jessica debated silently whether or not to tell Cara what was bothering her. What would she say? *Well, Cara, I'm depressed because I'm not as good a person as Liz. You know Liz, don't you? She's the one everyone likes.*

Jessica looked down at the table and shook her head. "It's nothing, Cara."

"Nothing?" she probed, her brown eyes flashing. "Or nothing you can talk about?"

"Nothing. Nothing," Jessica said flatly.

"Well," said Cara. "I'm in a terrific mood. I went to Foxy Mama's today and bought the most beautiful dress for the party. It's a peach color. Very short with a dropped waist. It cost a fortune, but it's worth it."

One of the waitresses came over and set down a tray with Cara's cheeseburger and fries.

"Thanks," Cara said, smiling. The girl smiled back and bustled away. "Take some fries if you want," Cara said to Jessica. "I'm supposed to be on a diet anyway."

"No, thanks." Jessica took another sip of her soda. "I had dinner just before I picked you up."

18

Jessica frowned, remembering the dinner and the argument with Steven. "Steve's home," she said to Cara.

"Oh, really? Well, that's nice."

It was no secret that Cara had been interested in Steven Wakefield for quite some time. Before Tricia Martin's death, Jessica had tried to set Cara up with her brother. Her plan had failed disastrously. Jessica could tell from the cool tone of Cara's voice that her friend was still upset with Steven.

"Oh, c'mon, Cara," Jessica said lightly, "you're not holding a grudge, are you?"

"No, Jess, I just don't want to be part of any of your schemes. "What's Steven doing home anyway? Is it his term break?"

Jessica gulped. She wasn't wild about having it spread all over Sweet Valley that her brother had left college. "I don't know," she lied. "Something like that."

"You *could* ask him to come to the party." Cara smiled, and Jessica noticed the gleam in her eye. She knew that Cara couldn't have gotten over Steven so quickly.

If she only knew, Jessica thought.

"Sure. I'll ask him, but I think he might be pretty busy with his schoolwork and all."

Jessica hoped Cara would let the subject drop there, and she was relieved when the sound of

19

voices at the door distracted Cara from the discussion.

"What's going on?" Jessica asked.

Cara leaned forward in her seat and tried to see the front of the restaurant. "I don't know. Mr. Doherty's talking to some people."

The voices got a little louder, and the girls could make out what was being said.

"Look, we just want to come in and get something to eat," a boy said.

"I don't want any trouble in here," said John Doherty.

"There isn't going to be any trouble," said someone else.

As John Doherty stepped back, Cara got a glimpse of the others at the front door.

"Looks like some of the crowd from the Shady Lady," Cara said.

The Shady Lady was a bar across the street from the Dairi Burger. It had a wild reputation, and the owners had recently gotten into trouble because of selling liquor to minors.

John Doherty was now talking to one of the boys in front. "All right, you can come in, but the first sign of any trouble and you're out. Understand?"

"Don't worry," the boy replied. "We just want something to eat."

Jessica couldn't see the front door from where she was sitting, so she had to rely on Cara for information. "Who's Mr. Doherty talking to?" she asked.

Cara smiled. "It's Nicky Shepard."

Jessica perked up. Nicky was also a junior at Sweet Valley High, and even though he didn't mix much with her friends, Jessica had always been intrigued by him. Nicky was wild, that was for sure. He spent a lot of time with the crowd from the Shady Lady and drove a fast car. There were also rumors about drugs. But there was something about him that fascinated Jessica. He was very good-looking in a rugged way. He wore his blond hair a little long, and he had pale blue eyes. His eyes were his most unusual feature. They were soft and sensitive-looking, in sharp contrast to the rest of his face.

Other than his physical appearance, Jessica knew little about Nicky Shepard. He was quiet most of the time, and his image at Sweet Valley High was that of a loner, cool and distant. He didn't play any sports, although he had the body of a football player.

Jessica turned and watched him walk to a nearby table with his friends. He carried himself like a natural leader. As he was sitting down, their eyes met for a second. He flashed Jessica a brilliant smile, and she felt a little charge of electricity run through her body. Without thinking about it, she smiled back.

"Jessica!" Cara snapped. "Why did you smile at him like that?"

"Because he smiled at me."

"Oh?" Cara said accusingly. She turned and glanced back at the table. "Well, you may have started something."

"What are you talking about?"

"He's still looking at you."

"Oh?" Jessica was the picture of innocence.

"Too bad he's in with that crowd," Cara said thoughtfully, as she popped a french fry into her mouth.

"That doesn't mean anything, Cara," Jessica said reproachfully. "I think he's sort of interesting, in a James Dean kind of way."

"You can't be serious, Jess." Cara laughed. "He's supposed to be into drugs."

"That's a rumor."

Cara rolled her eyes in exasperation.

Jessica smiled. "Anyway, Cara, you've got to admit Nicky's really good-looking."

"Yeah," Cara replied. "But so was Jack. Remember him?"

Jack Howard was a boy with whom both Jessica and Lila Fowler had fallen in love. An intense rivalry had developed between the two girls as they fought for Jack's attention. Neither one suspected, however, that despite his gorgeous appearance, Jack was a dangerous and terribly disturbed young man. After a violent confrontation with Jessica, Jack had been taken away from Sweet Valley for psychiatric care.

Jessica shuddered at the mention of Jack's name. Before she could comment that she was certain Nicky wasn't at all like Jack, Nicky got up and started over to their table. "Well, Cara," Jessica said, "if you don't want to be seen with him, you'd better take off. He's coming this way."

"Oh, no." Cara moaned.

Nicky walked over and stood at the edge of their table.

"Hi," he said to Jessica. His voice was surprisingly soft, even gentle. "You're one of the Wakefield clones, aren't you?"

"I don't care much for that word," Jessica said coldly.

Nicky smiled. "Mind if I join you?"

"Actually, yes," Cara snapped.

Nicky didn't even seem to notice. He sat down next to Jessica. "Really. Tell me, which one are you?"

"I'm the one who wants you to leave," Jessica replied.

Nicky rolled his eyes and winced. "Come on," he drawled. "You don't really want me to go."

"Yes, I do!" Jessica laughed.

"No, you don't."

He leaned closer to Jessica. "OK, look, if you

really want me to go, all you've got to say is, 'Nicky, please join my friend and me for a Coke,' and I'll go."

"I'm not going to say that," Jessica said. For some reason, she felt very nervous.

"Come on," Nicky insisted. "Just say it, and I'll go. I promise."

Jessica laughed. "I don't believe this." She glanced at Cara, who obviously wasn't amused. "Maybe I'll just call Mr. Doherty over and tell him you're bothering us."

"You won't do that." Nicky smiled.

"You think I won't?"

"No," he said, laughing. "I think you won't."

Jessica laughed again.

"See," Nicky touched her hand. She pulled it away quickly. "You don't really want me to go."

Jessica looked at him. "Nicky, join us for a Coke."

Nicky got up from the table. "Gee, I'd love to, but it would be rude for me to leave my friends. Maybe another time."

"Don't count on it," Cara said viciously.

Nicky kept his eyes on Jessica. "I don't count on anything. My life is a series of pleasant surprises."

"We're happy for you," Cara snapped.

He smiled his sexy smile again. "Nice talking to you, Jessica."

Jessica looked up at him. "How come you're sure I'm Jessica and not my sister?"

"Oh, I know a lot about you two." Nicky laughed. "You may look the same, but you're pretty different."

"How?" Jessica asked.

Nicky raised an eyebrow and smiled. "Your sister would never have asked me to stay." He grinned, "See you around."

Jessica watched him as he walked back to his friends.

Cara turned to Jessica, her dark eyes blazing, "Can you believe the nerve of that guy?"

Jessica's eyes sparkled, and she smiled slightly as she took a sip of her Tab.

She knew she should be angry at Nicky for his last remark, but somehow she was still attracted to him. Maybe even a little more so. Part of it was because, no matter how hard Nicky tried to be tough, his eyes gave him away. Jessica saw something in him that was even a little fragile—as if it would be easy to hurt him. No, Nicky wasn't like anyone she'd ever met before.

Besides, Jessica thought as she looked at Cara's face, it might be fun to shake her friends up a little. To show them that maybe they didn't know Jessica Wakefield as well as they thought they did.

Jessica smiled as she sipped her soda. Yes, Nicky Shepard was definitely worth checking out.

25

Three

Jessica had spent a full two hours getting ready for Cara's party.

And for what? she asked herself.

From her position near the food table, she could watch the party at Cara's, which was in full swing. The table was overloaded with hors d'oeuvres and dips. There were two kinds of punch in matching bowls at each end of the table, and all the usual chips and crackers.

The music was blaring in from the living room, and most of the Sweet Valley High crowd drifted around the rooms, laughing, dancing, and talking. Everyone was having a terrific time.

Everyone, that is, except Steven Wakefield.

After Elizabeth had explained to Steven that Jessica had nothing devious planned and was only trying to cheer him up, Steven had reluctantly agreed to come to the party. He'd apologized to Jessica in a halfhearted way and had driven her to Cara's in absolute silence. As soon as he entered, he said hello to a few people, poured a glass of punch, and placed himself in a chair in the corner. He had spent the whole evening in that chair, slumped over and frowning. Twice Cara had asked him to dance, but Steven had said he wasn't in the mood.

Jessica was fuming. Couldn't Steven see he was embarrassing her in front of all her friends? Jessica wished Elizabeth had kept her goody-goody mouth shut.

Sure, it's fine for Liz, Jessica brooded. *She's having a wonderful time with good old Todd. She hasn't even checked on Steve once since she arrived. But I have to stand here all night and watch him being depressed. It just isn't fair. If he's so miserable, why doesn't he just go home?*

Just about everyone seemed to be having a great time. Elizabeth and Todd were dancing up a storm alongside Ken Matthews and Cara. Aaron Dallas, John Pfeifer, and Tony Esteban were off discussing sports. In one corner a group of people were playing Trivial Pursuit.

Everyone else is having a wonderful time, Jessica complained silently. *Nobody else is stuck with a morose brother for a date.*

What bothered Jessica most was how quickly Steven had responded to Elizabeth's invitation. Once again, her twin had stepped in and smoothed everything over after Jessica had botched it up. Jessica was furious that her twin seemingly could do no wrong and that nothing she herself tried ever seemed to turn out right.

Jessica was suddenly pulled from her thoughts by Caroline Pearce, who came running up to the food table, flushed and laughing after several vigorous dances with Jerry Fisher, her boyfriend from Woodgrove, a town about an hour's drive from Sweet Valley. Jessica still marveled whenever she saw Caroline with the dark-haired basketball player.

It was only a short while before that Caroline had been a misfit who was tolerated by Jessica's crowd only because she was great at passing on gossip. Recently Caroline had undergone a major change with some help from Elizabeth. She had become sweeter, more relaxed, and no longer gossiped about anyone. Jessica noted to herself that Caroline even looked prettier. Her soft, ivory skin seemed to glow from within, and the green jumpsuit she was wearing set off her red hair and green eyes dramatically.

Oh, well, Jessica muttered to herself, *Elizabeth Wakefield, savior of the world, defender of the oppressed, strikes again.*

"Hi, Jess," Caroline called brightly as she

29

approached the table, Jerry in tow. "Isn't this party just fabulous?"

"Fabulous," Jessica said unenthusiastically.

But Caroline didn't catch the sarcasm in Jessica's voice. "You look so pretty, Jess," she continued. "I love that dress." Caroline touched the fabric of the loose, gray silk shift Jessica was wearing.

"Thanks." For once, Jessica wasn't in the mood for compliments.

"Liz looks wonderful, too," Caroline gushed.

Jessica didn't even try to cover the bitterness in her voice. "Doesn't she always?"

"Yeah," the redhead agreed enthusiastically. "You don't know how lucky you are to have a sister like Elizabeth, Jess. I never knew what a real friend was before her."

Elizabeth Wakefield, everyone's best friend, Jessica added to her list of silent complaints about her twin.

The music changed, and Jerry grabbed Caroline's arm. "Come on! They're playing that song I like."

"See ya, Jess," Caroline called over her shoulder as Jerry pulled her back to the dance floor.

Jessica took another look at Steven, who was still alone in the chair in the corner. *He could at least ask me to dance*, she thought bitterly. But no matter how hard she tried, she couldn't catch her brother's eye. Finally she gave up and decided to go outside and get some air.

Jessica made her way through the crowd to the hallway. She was heading toward the back door when she met Elizabeth and Todd.

"Hi, Jess." Todd smiled. As usual, he and Elizabeth looked perfect together. Todd was wearing pleated gray linen slacks and a tweed coat over a polo shirt. Elizabeth looked especially pretty in her new blue blouse and a white skirt. Her golden hair, which she usually wore in a simple ponytail, was pulled in a tight French braid.

"How's Steve doing?" Elizabeth asked her twin warily.

"Oh, wonderfully," Jessica answered brightly. "He's the life of the party."

Elizabeth smiled. "Great. I knew this was all he needed." She grabbed Todd's hand and placed it in Jessica's. "Here. Do me a favor, little sister. Watch this hunk while I run off to the bathroom. I don't want anyone stealing him while I'm gone."

"Actually, I was just—"

Jessica's words were ignored as Todd wrapped his arms around Elizabeth.

"You'd better hurry. I don't know how long Jess can hold them all off," he quipped.

Elizabeth smiled and turned her face up to his. She kissed him tenderly. "Help her out a little. OK?"

Todd returned the kiss. "No problem."

This is so sweet, thought Jessica. *I'm getting sick.*

31

Elizabeth ran off.

"Your sister is really something." Todd watched Elizabeth disappear.

"Oh, she's something else, all right," Jessica said.

"Do you know what she said to me awhile ago?"

Jessica cut him off bitterly. "Something wonderfully sweet and profound, I'm sure!"

Todd drew back a step, looking confused.

"Look, Todd," Jessica went on, "I'm sure you have nothing but the highest regard for my dear sister, but right now, I'd appreciate it if you would keep it to yourself. Now, if you don't mind, I'm going out for some air."

She turned abruptly and went down the hall. In the kitchen she pushed her way through the crowd that had gathered there, then went out the back door.

Angry and hurt, Jessica stormed into the night air. In the back part of the lawn was a small bathhouse, where people changed for the pool. Jessica headed for it. Normally, she didn't enjoy being alone. But given a choice between being by herself and listening to praise being heaped on her twin, she preferred being alone.

She got to the bathhouse and opened the door. It was dark inside. She decided not to turn on the light. That would just invite more people out there.

Jessica turned as she shut the door. The bathhouse was about the size of her room at home. In the moonlight she could see the dark wood floor and some wicker furniture.

"Well, I wasn't expecting company," said a soft male voice.

Jessica was startled. She jumped and scanned the dark room to see where the voice was coming from. In the corner she could make out a figure on the chaise longe.

Jessica turned back to the door. "Sorry, I didn't know there was anybody out here."

"There isn't. Just me." She could hear the creak of wicker as the boy sat up. "Come in and sit down. It's Jessica, isn't it?"

Jessica strained to see in the darkness. A small lamp next to the chaise snapped on to reveal Nicky Shepard smiling at her.

"I didn't know you were invited to the party." Jessica tried to conceal the excitement in her voice. She had been trying to figure out a way to get to know Nicky better, and here it had fallen into her lap.

"Oh, I came with Dana and Guy." Nicky continued to smile as he mentioned the names of two of The Droids, Sweet Valley High's premier rock band.

"They're friends of yours?"

"Sort of." Nicky motioned to a chair near his. "Sit down."

Jessica smiled and walked to the chair. She sat down and crossed her legs. "So, how come you're out here?"

"How come *you're* out here?"

"I asked you first."

Nicky smiled at her again, and Jessica felt a little chill run up her spine. He was so good-looking. His sun-blond hair was brushed back from his face, and his light blue eyes looked even more striking in the semi-darkness.

"That's right," he said, laughing. "OK. I don't do very well at parties."

"So you like to spend your time at them off by yourself?" Jessica decided to keep her distance for now. She was interested in Nicky, but she was still a little afraid of him.

"I like being a loner," he said in a low voice. "It makes me seem mysterious."

"It makes you seem sad," Jessica replied.

"Maybe I like being sad."

"How can you like being sad?" Jessica asked honestly.

"It's easier than being happy."

Jessica felt even more intrigued. She leaned forward and rested her head on her hands. "What makes you sad, Nicky?"

Nicky looked straight into her eyes. "You don't like me, do you?"

34

His question flustered her. "I never said that," she said hastily.

"You don't have to say it." He smiled. "I can tell. I'm not your kind."

"What kind is that?" Jessica asked defensively.

"Why don't we just drop it?"

"I don't want to drop it. What did you mean?"

"OK, what kind? The kind that everything goes right for."

Jessica was going to protest, but Nicky didn't give her a chance. He went right on talking. "The kind of guy who loves this whole high school thing. The kind who gets all the breaks, nice friends, parents who care. The kind who ends up with all the marbles at the end of the game."

Jessica couldn't have left now if she wanted to. "You think your parents don't care about you," she said. It was a statement, not a question.

Nicky pulled a cigarette out of his pocket and lit it. He tossed the match into an ashtray. "Oh, I suppose they would if they had the time." He leaned forward and stared at the wooden floor. The smoke from the cigarette curled up around his face, making a soft, yellow-gray haze around his head. "My dad . . . my dad. He's an American dream. He was poor when he was a kid, and he's worked all his life to get where he is now. The problem is, he's so busy making himself, I'm surprised he had the time to make me in the first place. And then, there's my

35

mom," he went on. "She's busy, too. See, my younger brother, Danny, has a lot of health problems. Asthma and stuff. It doesn't give her much time for a healthy kid like me."

Jessica could see Nicky's pain, and she was touched by it. "Maybe you should talk to them about it."

Nicky laughed. "Why? I like it like this. I can do pretty much anything I want to. Nobody cares. Nobody bothers me. I'm free."

"I'm sure your parents care about you, even if they don't show it."

Nicky looked up at her. "Why?"

Jessica was puzzled. "Why, what?"

"Why are you sure?"

"Well"—Jessica fumbled for words—"everybody's parents care about them."

Nicky laughed again, this time a short, bitter laugh. "Oh, yeah? What television show have you been living in?"

"My life isn't so perfect, you know," Jessica replied defensively.

Nicky's eyebrows arched in mock concern. "Really? Why don't you tell me about it, Jessica?"

Jessica stood up and went to the door. "It's nothing I care to discuss with you."

Nicky laughed. "See? I was right."

Jessica turned. "About what?"

"You don't like me."

"I don't dislike you."

"You wouldn't feel so terrific about it if some of your friends came in right now and saw you talking to me, would you?"

"I don't care about what they think," Jessica lied.

"Don't give me that, Ms. Co-captain-of-the-cheerleading-squad." Nicky smiled. "You're so concerned with what you think you should be that you don't even know who you are."

"Oh, yeah?" Jessica's voice was a little less controlled. "Why don't you tell me who I am, if you know so much."

Nicky ground the cigarette out in an ashtray near the chaise. "OK. First of all, you're about the most beautiful girl I've ever seen. You're smart, too. Smarter than they all realize. You always know exactly what you want and exactly how to get it, and it doesn't matter a bit who gets in the way. You're not afraid of anything. Except me," he added slyly.

Jessica laughed nervously. "I'm not afraid of you."

"You're also a pretty good liar," Nicky said quietly. "But not good enough."

Jessica sat back down and tried to look amused. "Why would I be afraid of you?"

Nicky looked her straight in the eye and spoke in dead earnest. "Because you're so much like me."

It got very still in the bathhouse, and the silence

37

hung in the air. Nicky leaned back in the chaise and crossed his arms over his chest. He slowly broke into a smile, a smile that was infectious, and before long, Jessica joined him in laughter.

"You know," Jessica said, flashing Nicky her brightest smile, "you're really a nice person."

Nicky returned the smile. "You know, so are you."

Nicky stared at her for a moment in silence. "Close your eyes." He sat up on the chaise.

Jessica eyed him suspiciously. "What for?"

"Just close your eyes. Come on. Trust me."

Jessica wasn't quite sure that was a good idea. She thought about it for a moment and then closed her eyes.

It seemed as if she had had them closed forever, although it must have been only a second or two. She heard the creak of wicker as Nicky got up from his seat, and then, even though she expected it, she jumped as his lips softly touched hers. It was just one kiss, but it was a beautiful one, warm and tender.

Nicky broke the kiss first, and when Jessica opened her eyes, he was seated on the chaise again.

"That was nice," she said softly.

Nicky just smiled. Although she had been nervous around him at first, Jessica discovered that she was now feeling at ease. She felt very calm, and her company seemed to open him up. More and more, Jessica found the rumors about Nicky harder to believe.

"Want to go back in?" He stood and offered her his arm.

"I thought you didn't like parties?"

"I feel like dancing. How about you?"

Jessica smiled at him tenderly. She stood and took the arm he offered. "It would be a pleasure, sir."

He kissed her once again as they walked out of the little house and back to the party.

From the way she'd seen him move, Jessica thought Nicky might be a good dancer, but she wasn't prepared for how good he really was. They spent a solid hour on the dance floor, completely lost in each other and the music. Nicky was one of the best dancers Jessica had ever seen, and their movements together were smooth and natural.

The appearance of Jessica on the dance floor with Nicky caused a stir at the party. Nicky had always been so quiet and withdrawn that he didn't seem to be the kind of person Jessica Wakefield would be attracted to. Yet, as odd as it seemed, they danced every dance together and looked like much more than friends.

Elizabeth and Todd were sitting in the den, drinking punch and watching music videos, when

Lila Fowler breezed into the room and flopped down on a chair across from them. She fanned her face and giggled quietly as she caught her breath.

"Well, someone's been pouring it on," Elizabeth said, laughing.

Lila wiped her brow with the edge of the purple scarf she was wearing around her neck. "You bet! This is the first chance I've had to sit down all evening."

Elizabeth checked her watch. "Well, it's getting kind of late. Things should start to cool off soon."

Lila smiled wickedly. "Not with the way Jessica is going."

Elizabeth looked at Lila quizzically. She hadn't seen her sister for quite a while and had no idea what Lila was talking about.

"What?" Elizabeth asked. "Are she and my brother giving dancing lessons?"

"Oh, she's dancing all right." Lila pulled out a small makeup mirror and checked her lipstick. "But not with Steve."

From the tone of Lila's voice, Elizabeth knew her twin was up to something. She excused herself and walked into the other room.

Well, this is something for "Eyes and Ears," Elizabeth decided, thinking about the gossip column she wrote for *The Oracle*. It was usually filled with items about the students at Sweet Valley High: who was running for what, who was dating

40

whom, anything that could be considered newsworthy.

And Jessica Wakefield, looking more than a little romantic with Nicky Shepard, was definitely newsworthy.

When Elizabeth entered the room, a slow song was playing on the stereo, and Jessica was wrapped in a tight embrace with Nicky as they swayed to the music. Elizabeth didn't know much about Nicky Shepard. She had hardly ever talked to him. Of course, she had heard all the rumors, but Elizabeth had never put too much faith in rumors.

Still, it was strange. Jessica normally would never have been seen with someone like Nicky, someone who wasn't popular and well liked. And the group Nicky hung out with was definitely *not* well liked.

Jessica hadn't noticed her sister watching her. She was too caught up in the dance.

Nicky put his head closer to hers and whispered in her ear. "Want to take off?"

"Why?" Jessica whispered back. "Aren't you having a good time here?"

"Of course I am. I just thought it might be nice to be alone for a while."

Jessica looked up into Nicky's eyes. *It sure would*, she thought to herself.

Just then she caught sight of Elizabeth. "OK."

She smiled at Nicky. "Just give me a second to tell Liz where I'm going."

She broke away from him and walked over to her twin. "Hi, Liz," she said brightly. "Having fun?"

"Well, I must say, Jessica, dear, you never fail to surprise me."

Jessica smiled innocently. "Oh? How's that?"

"You and Nicky Shepard."

"Isn't he beautiful?"

Elizabeth eyed her sister cautiously. "He *is* good-looking, Jess, but you really don't know much about him, do you?"

Jessica could have guessed that Elizabeth's question was coming. Once again, Elizabeth was acting as though she had to watch over her "little" sister. *Well*, thought Jessica, *I may be four minutes younger, but I am fully capable of looking out for myself.*

"I know enough," Jessica said coldly. "And I'm finding out more all the time."

Elizabeth recognized her sister's tone of voice. It meant that Jessica had said all she was going to say. She also heard an edge to Jessica's voice that she had been hearing a lot lately, an edge that sounded a lot like resentment.

"Jess, are you mad at me about something?" she asked.

"Don't be silly, Liz," Jessica said sarcastically. "Why would anyone be mad at you? You're perfect."

42

The twins stared at each other for a moment in uncomfortable silence. Finally, Elizabeth decided to try a different tactic.

"Look, the real reason I came over is to remind you that it's getting a little late. Steve might want to take off."

"Tell him to go ahead," Jessica replied. She had had enough of looking out for Steven that night. "Nicky and I are going out for something to eat. He'll drive me home."

"Jess," Elizabeth protested. "You hardly know Nicky. Do you think you should—"

"Liz." Jessica cut her twin off. "I'm old enough to take care of myself. You've got the rest of the world to watch out for. Don't worry so much about me."

Before Elizabeth could reply, Jessica walked back over to Nicky and grabbed his hand. "Come on," she said. "Let's go."

They had gotten halfway to Nicky's car when Jessica realized she'd forgotten her sweater in Cara's bedroom. She sent Nicky ahead and ran back into the house to get it. She grabbed the sweater and was out the front door again when Steven caught up with her.

"Hey, Jess," Steven said. Jessica stopped and turned to face him. "Liz tells me you're taking off."

"Yes," Jessica replied. "A friend is taking me out for something to eat. He'll give me a ride home."

"Hey, look, a bunch of us are going for pizza. Maybe you and your friend would like to join us."

Jessica eyed Steven suspiciously. "Whose idea was that? Elizabeth's?"

"Well, yeah, but . . ."

"I thought so."

"We just thought—" Steven was getting a little flustered. "Look, Jess, we're just worried about you."

"Well, don't be, OK? I mean, isn't that the way you wanted it? You don't meddle in my life, and I won't meddle in yours. OK?"

Both of them turned as they heard Nicky revving up his car, an old Mustang, racked up in the back.

"Look, I've got to go," Jessica said. She turned and ran to the car.

"Jess," Steven called after her, but it was no use. Jessica had already climbed into the car. A moment later she and Nicky disappeared down the driveway.

Four

Elizabeth looked across the brunch table at her parents. Steven hadn't come downstairs yet, and neither had Jessica, who hadn't gotten home until after one o'clock that morning.

Jessica's attitude the previous evening had stuck with Elizabeth for the rest of the night, and it bothered her. She had noticed for some time that Jessica had been withdrawing. At times Jessica seemed less lively than usual; other times she seemed more sensitive, almost touchy.

The resentment Elizabeth sensed from her twin disturbed her. She felt it was about time she got some advice on the subject, so she'd made it a point to get downstairs early enough to discuss it with her parents.

"The problem is," Elizabeth ended after

describing the situation, "I don't think any of us really takes Jessica's moods seriously."

"I don't know," her mother said, helping herself to another pancake. "I agree that Jess isn't herself these days, but I think it's a change for the better. She seems more in control to me. No complaints, no arguments—"

"That's just what I mean," Elizabeth interrupted. "It may be nice, but it just isn't Jessica."

"Oh, I'm sure it's just boy trouble," her father said. "That's what it usually is."

The talk ended when Jessica entered the kitchen. "Good morning," she said listlessly as she sat at her place. She speared two pancakes and covered them with butter and syrup.

"Late night," her father said to her.

Jessica began eating. "Um-hm," she agreed.

Her mother filled her glass with orange juice. "So, did you have a good time?"

"Oh, yeah," Jessica replied.

"How about Steve?" her father asked warily.

Elizabeth frowned. "No. I don't think Steve had a very good time," she answered.

Her father sighed. "Well, I thought he and I could spend some time together today. Maybe that will bring him out of it."

Jessica said nothing. She just sat, staring down at the table as she ate.

Elizabeth watched her twin. She was getting a little angry that her parents weren't more concerned about the change in Jessica.

Jessica looked up. "Has Steve been down yet?"

"No. Not yet," her mother answered.

Jessica turned to Elizabeth. "Liz, what are you doing today?"

"I was going to go over to Todd's."

"Are you taking the car?"

Elizabeth finished her breakfast and folded her napkin. "I had planned on it."

Jessica shrugged her shoulders. "OK."

This was just what Elizabeth had been talking about. She shot a glance at her parents. Normally Jessica would have pulled something if she wanted the car. It just wasn't natural for her to be so compliant.

"I can get Todd to give me a ride if you need the car," Elizabeth offered.

Jessica pushed her plate away. "No, it's OK."

"Really, Jess, it's no problem."

Jessica shook her head. "No. It's not important."

There was silence at the table for a second. Alice and Ned Wakefield exchanged a look that told Elizabeth they were beginning to see what she had been talking about.

Their mother put down her fork and turned to Jessica. "Jess, is something wrong?" she asked.

Jessica was quiet for a moment, then she looked up. "No. Nothing's wrong," she said brightly.

"You seem a little quiet," her father offered, not fooled by Jessica's act.

Jessica smiled. "I'm just tired, I guess."

Mr. Wakefield decided to let the matter drop. If Jessica was having problems, she would tell them about it when she wanted to. "Well," he said, getting up from the table, "I'm going to go see if I can interest your brother in a little tennis."

"That sounds good."

Their mother smiled brightly. "I could go for that myself. Want to make it doubles, Jessica?"

Jessica smiled halfheartedly. "No, I don't think so. Maybe later." She began clearing off the brunch dishes. "You can all go ahead. I'll take care of this."

Their mother and father got up from the table and left the room, but Elizabeth remained sitting, staring at her twin as she cleared off the table.

"What did you do last night after you left?" Elizabeth asked.

Jessica didn't look at Elizabeth. She just went to the sink and began rinsing the dishes. "Nothing. You know, we got something to eat, and then he took me home."

It was quiet in the kitchen for a second, and it was clear that Jessica didn't want to talk. But Elizabeth wasn't about to be put off by her sister's attitude. "What's he like?"

"Who?"

"Nicky."

Jessica didn't turn around. "He's OK. He's not as bad as everyone thinks he is. Really, he's just a little confused."

There was another awkward pause filled only by the sound of water rushing into the sink.

Elizabeth tried again. "Look, Jess, if you want the car, really, it's no problem for Todd to pick me up."

"Don't worry about it," Jessica snapped. "I'd probably just get into trouble with it."

"Why would you say something like that?" Elizabeth's concern showed in her voice, but it only succeeded in irritating Jessica further.

"Look, Liz." Jessica turned and faced her sister. "Can't you figure it out?"

"Figure out what?"

"Come on, Liz." Jessica was rolling now. "You're so perfect, can't you see that I'm just coming to the realization that nobody in this family wants me around?"

Elizabeth felt as if the wind had been knocked out of her. "That's just not true, Jess."

"Oh, no?" For a moment, Jessica was tempted to let loose all her pent-up feelings. But she caught herself. It wouldn't make any difference anyway. She could never make Elizabeth understand how she felt.

"I'm sorry, Liz." Jessica turned her attention to

loading the dishwasher. "I just didn't get much sleep last night. I guess I'm a little jumpy."

Elizabeth watched her twin carefully as she busied herself with the dishes. She could see that Jessica wanted to drop the subject, and maybe it was for the better. Maybe Jessica was just in a bad mood, and it would pass.

"Want me to help?" Elizabeth asked as she picked up a rinsed plate.

"Sure."

Jessica nodded at her twin and smiled, but didn't say another word. There was an uncomfortable silence as the two girls finished the dishes.

Much as she tried to dismiss it, Elizabeth knew that something was bothering Jessica. Something important. She also knew that, for once, she couldn't get through to her twin to talk about it. And this time she didn't know what to do.

Five

"I think it's really serious this time, Steve," Elizabeth said on Monday afternoon as she and her brother walked in front of the bright shop windows that lined either side of the mall. "I've never seen her like this."

Elizabeth hadn't spoken about the incident in the kitchen to anyone. She hadn't even mentioned it to Todd the day before, even though he'd noticed she seemed preoccupied all day. She knew Todd wasn't Jessica's biggest fan, and she didn't feel she could confide in him about something this serious. She didn't even know how to bring it up to her parents. So Steven was the only one left.

"I think you're right, Liz," Steven agreed. Elizabeth noticed that for the first time since he'd been home, Steven seemed to be concerned about something other than his own problems. In spite of

51

Steven and Jessica's bickering, Elizabeth knew he really cared about their sister.

"Maybe I should talk to her," Steven offered. "I feel sort of guilty about how I jumped on her about Cara's party."

"It's OK," Elizabeth comforted her brother.

Steven smiled sadly. "I've just had a lot on my mind lately. I don't know. I'm a little confused, but that didn't give me the right to attack Jessica like I did. She was trying to help."

Steven had been in a good mood all afternoon, and Elizabeth didn't want him to sink back down again. "You didn't know. Anyway, yes, I think it's a good idea for you to have a talk with her. Maybe she'll listen to you. I've tried to talk to her, but I just can't seem to say anything right."

Steven gave her a hug. "Don't worry about it," he said brightly. "Jess didn't mean all that stuff she said. It's just something she's going through right now."

Elizabeth nodded and smiled, even though she wasn't sure that what he had said was true.

"Hey," Steven said suddenly. "How would you react if a large hot-fudge sundae walked up to you right now and said hello?"

Elizabeth laughed. "Well, let's see. . . . I guess I'd say, 'Pleasure to eat you!' "

"Well, my girl"—Steve grabbed her hand and pulled her into Casey's, the ice-cream parlor in the mall—"let me introduce you to one right this minute."

They took a table near the front, and Steven handed his sister one of the menus that was on the table. As Elizabeth looked over the choices, her concern about Jessica let up a bit.

Good old Steve, she thought. *He really knows how to get my mind off something.*

Behind the counter, the waiter had his back turned to them. He appeared to be deep in thought as he polished a glass.

"Hello," Steven called to him.

Elizabeth smiled brightly when he turned, and she saw that the waiter was Ricky Capaldo.

Ricky returned the smile unenthusiastically. "Hi, Liz," he said, walking to their table.

Ricky was the manager of the Sweet Valley High cheerleading squad and was one of Elizabeth's favorite people. In spite of his shyness, his warm brown eyes always seemed to be friendly and smiling. He wasn't smiling now, though. Elizabeth hoped nothing was wrong between him and his girlfriend, Annie Whitman. *It would be a shame if those two broke up,* she thought to herself. Especially after all they'd been through together. Ricky had stuck by Annie when rumors about her bad reputation were circulating around Sweet Valley High. It was Ricky who had rushed Annie to the hospital after she attempted suicide, and Ricky who stayed by her bed constantly until she came out of her coma and was well again. They had been inseparable after that, and it was hard for Elizabeth to believe that anything could pull them apart.

She smiled brightly at him. "Hi, Ricky. I didn't know you worked here."

Ricky shrugged. "I just started last week."

Again Elizabeth noticed that Ricky seemed distracted and sad.

Elizabeth took a deep breath. "How's Annie?"

For the first time that afternoon, Ricky's face brightened, and Elizabeth saw a bit of the Ricky she knew from school. "Oh, she's fine. Really great."

"I didn't get to talk to you two at Cara's party the other night. What's she doing with her week off?"

"Just getting some sun, I think," Ricky replied.

Steven cleared his throat.

"Oh, I'm sorry," Elizabeth said. "I don't think you know my brother, Steve. Steve, this is Ricky Capaldo."

The two of them nodded and exchanged hellos. Ricky held his order pad up a little higher and tapped the point of a pencil against it. "So! What's it gonna be?"

Elizabeth bit her lip. "I don't know. I guess a hot-fudge sundae with double-fudge ice cream."

"Don't like chocolate much, do you?" Steven laughed. "What the heck, I'll have the same."

"Right." Ricky finished writing the order and brought it back to the counter.

"He seems like a nice guy," Steven said.

"He is," Elizabeth agreed. "He doesn't seem like himself today, though. Usually he's a lot friendlier." She watched Ricky as he took orders from the other tables. It did seem as if his mind was elsewhere.

"Well, maybe he just doesn't feel friendly today," Steven offered.

Ricky returned to the table a few minutes later with the two sundaes. "Here we are." He put them down with a flourish. "Paradise in a bowl."

Elizabeth's eyes bugged out at the sight of the heaping mounds of rich, dark ice cream, topped with steaming hot fudge and a dollop of whipped cream.

"I guess so," she replied. But a moment later, even the wonderful treat couldn't keep her worries about Jessica from returning.

Steven seemed able to read her mind. "Don't worry about Jess. I'll talk to her. Everything's going to be all right."

I hope so, Elizabeth thought, *I sincerely hope so*.

"Elizabeth Wakefield!" a friendly voice called. "Mind if we join you?"

Elizabeth glanced up in surprise, her spoon frozen halfway to her mouth. "Come on over!" she said enthusiastically, sliding over in the booth to make more room as Bill Chase and his girl friend DeeDee Gordon approached.

Elizabeth introduced the couple to Steven. "Bill's a champion surfer," Elizabeth said. "And DeeDee is a terrific artist."

As the couple sat down, Elizabeth reflected that her hasty introductions didn't really do either Bill or DeeDee justice. Bill was a tall, athletic blond whose surfing trophies had won him a spot in the junior class's hall of fame. More recently, he'd become increasingly involved in acting. In fact, he had his own agent—and dreams of taking up the theater as a career once he finished school.

DeeDee looked even more petite and cute than usual. Her brown hair was sleek and smooth, and her pale complexion was sprinkled with a light dusting of freckles. Elizabeth didn't know DeeDee very well, but she'd worked with her on a number of projects at school and had always found her a pleasure to be with. Sparkling, lighthearted, filled with ideas—that was DeeDee Gordon.

"Enid told me you're taking design courses at the Civic Center," Elizabeth said to DeeDee now, remembering how delighted Enid had been that the spunky brunette was finally getting professional instruction to develop a talent people had noticed for years. "How are you finding them? Are they useful?"

To her amazement, DeeDee turned bright red

and looked down at the table. "I—uh, I decided not to continue taking the classes," she muttered, her face flaming.

Elizabeth felt completely confused. Obviously she had upset DeeDee, and she had no idea what she had said wrong.

Her discomfort increased as Bill turned on DeeDee, obviously hearing this piece of news for the first time. "What are you talking about?" he demanded, his handsome face darkening. "Dee, you've been talking about those courses for months! Why'd you decide to bag them now?"

Boy, Elizabeth thought, catching her brother's eye and shrugging at his quizzical expression, *I sure keep striking out these days!*

First Jessica had given Elizabeth the cold shoulder. And then Ricky Capaldo. And then she'd asked DeeDee Gordon a perfectly innocent question, and all hell had broken loose!

Elizabeth sighed and pushed her sundae away. Suddenly she didn't have quite the appetite for it she'd felt several minutes earlier.

"We'll talk about this later," Bill was saying under his breath to DeeDee. An unnatural smile on his face, he turned back to Elizabeth and Steven, obviously trying to make everything look normal again.

But Elizabeth could tell from the strained look on his face that something was really bugging him.

57

And DeeDee, she thought sympathetically, looked absolutely miserable!

Elizabeth had enough on her mind right now as it was. But she couldn't help wondering what was going on with the couple.

It was kind of funny, she thought, pulling her sundae back and deciding to give it one more try. Enid had been convinced that Bill and DeeDee were one of the happiest couples she'd ever seen.

But from the way they were just glaring at each other, Elizabeth was not so sure!

Jessica pulled herself onto the diving board. She lay very still on her back and let the sun dry the drops of water that beaded on her legs and arms. The sun was hot, and the cool water of the Wakefield pool had felt wonderful.

Suddenly something blocked out the sun. She opened her eyes and saw her brother Steven standing over her.

"Hi," she said to him. "Finish shopping already?"

"Yeah." He smiled. "We were kind of surprised you didn't come along. Normally, nothing short of a broken leg can keep you from spending money."

Jessica laughed. "Well, I just didn't feel like it, I guess."

Steven sat down next to the board. "Mind if I sit here for a while? I think we need to talk."

Jessica pulled a towel over her eyes. "Oh? About what?"

"I just—I've noticed that something seems to be wrong between you and Liz," he said after a moment.

Jessica turned her head away slightly. "Nothing's wrong."

"Yeah. Well—it seems like you two aren't as close as you usually are." Steven waited for a reply, but Jessica was silent. "Of course, maybe it's none of my business."

"Maybe you're right," Jessica said.

Steven was taken aback. "Jessica—"

"What?"

"You really seem down lately. It's not like you."

Again Jessica said nothing. Steven began to get frustrated. "Talk to me, Jess. Look, I'm sorry about the way I snapped at you when you first mentioned Cara's party. I shouldn't have spoken to you like that, but, see, I haven't really been myself these last few weeks, and I thought you were trying to push Cara on me again."

Jessica sat up. The towel dropped to her lap.

"Did Elizabeth tell you to come out here and talk to me?"

"No," Steven lied.

Jessica gave her brother an icy stare.

"So what if she did?" he asked defensively. He

felt himself getting annoyed with his sister, and he tried to fight the feeling.

"I knew it," Jessica muttered.

"Look, Jessica." Steven tried hard to keep what he was feeling out of his voice. "It's just that I've noticed you seem depressed lately, and you aren't talking to any of us."

"I thought that was what you wanted."

"Come on, Jess. I said I was sorry about the Cara thing. I just didn't understand what you were trying to do, and I got mad."

"You would never have gotten mad if Liz suggested it. If *she* had been trying to fix you up with somebody, you would have thought it was a great idea."

Steven's patience was at the breaking point. "Liz would never have tried something like that," he said, his voice rising angrily.

"See?" Jessica snapped. "There it is. That's how you really feel, isn't it?"

Steven felt the conversation slipping away from him, and he couldn't stop it. "Jess. I didn't want this to turn out this way."

"What did you want, Steve?" Jessica spat out. "Did you come out here to do some more missionary work on Jessica? Well, it isn't working!"

Steven stood up. "That isn't the way it is, Jess, and you know it."

"I may be a lot of things, Steve, but I'm not stupid." Jessica lay back down and covered her face again with the towel.

Steven stood looking at her silently for a moment. There was nothing else he could say. He felt awkward and stupid. He had come outside wanting to help Jessica, but she wasn't having it.

"Look, Jess," he finally said. "You're my sister, just as much as Elizabeth is, and I love you just as much as I love her. When you're ready to believe that, we'll talk again."

He waited for a moment, hoping for a reply. When Jessica said nothing, he walked away from the pool and went back into the house.

A moment later Jessica flung the towel off and dived into the pool, hot tears stinging her eyes. She swam underwater for as long as she could. It seemed like forever. At the other end of the pool, she lifted herself out of the water and dropped to her stomach on the warm grass. She lay there quietly and caught her breath.

She knew she was being unfair to Steven. She knew she was saying all the wrong things even as the words were leaving her mouth. Why couldn't she just have accepted his offer of friendship? Why couldn't she make them see how she felt?

Maybe she could.

The whole problem, Jessica thought, was that her family thought Elizabeth was so much better than she was. *But I can change. Maybe, if I could show them that I'm turning over a new leaf* . . .

Jessica thought about ways of changing. She could start by cleaning up her room. No, she thought, frowning, she needed to show them something immediately. Even she had to admit that it would take a full day to get her room in order.

Well, she could at least make dinner. She briefly thought about her last attempt to surprise her family with dinner. She had tried an elaborate seafood salad but had succeeded only in making Elizabeth and her parents sick. Jessica shook her head and resolved to show them that she'd undergone some big changes since then.

With a determined look, she headed for the kitchen.

Alice Wakefield couldn't believe her eyes as she entered the kitchen.

Dinner was ready. There was a roast chicken waiting to be carved. Rice and vegetables were steaming on the stove, and presiding over the whole affair, from her point of command in front of the stove, was none other than Jessica.

Holding a wooden spoon in one hand, she turned to her mother and smiled. "Hi," she called brightly. "Dinner's almost ready, but you've got time for a glass of wine if you like."

Her mother was almost speechless. She put her purse and briefcase on the counter. "Sure. That would be nice."

Jessica walked over to the counter and poured her mother a glass of chilled white wine.

"I thought it was my turn to make dinner," Alice Wakefield said, walking over to inspect the chicken. She was trying to be as diplomatic as possible, but the memory of Jessica's last venture into the world of cooking was still vivid in her mind.

"It was," Jessica said, checking on the vegetables. "But I thought you might be tired after working all day."

Alice Wakefield looked around. She was in the right kitchen, and this was her daughter Jessica. "Did you make sure the chicken was completely thawed before putting it in the oven?"

"Of course," Jessica replied. She knew what was on her mother's mind. "Don't worry," she said. "I'm not going to poison you all again."

Her mother smiled uncomfortably and started to put on an apron. "I'll just give you a hand finishing up in here."

"No, no, no." Jessica took the apron from her mother and turned her toward the door. "I don't need any help. Honest." She pushed her mother all the way through the door and pointed her to the living room. "Just go into the living room and talk to that handsome husband of yours. I'll call you when everything's ready."

"Sure," Mrs. Wakefield said tentatively. "I'll just go in and set the table first."

"It's all done," Jessica replied. "Just go in and sit down."

Alice Wakefield stared at her daughter's back for a second. The theme music from "The Twilight Zone" began to play softly in her head. She toyed with the idea that maybe she'd wandered into another dimension. Then she shook her head, took a sip of the wine, and went in to join her husband.

Ned Wakefield was sitting in the living room, a glass of wine in his hand and a puzzled expression on his face. He looked up at his wife when she walked into the room.

"It's not a car because we just gave them the car," he said, "but it has to be something big."

Alice Wakefield laughed as she sat next to him. "No, just because Jessica made dinner doesn't mean that she wants something. Maybe we're not really being fair."

He gave her a kiss on the cheek. "You're right. I'm not being fair."

"Jessica always pulls her weight around here," she went on, "and just because she's doing a little more than her share tonight it doesn't necessarily mean she wants something."

Ned Wakefield nodded thoughtfully. "That's true."

Alice Wakefield sipped her wine and stared into the glass. "But whatever it is, I hope we can afford it."

The two were laughing as Jessica called them to dinner.

Elizabeth and Steven were already at the table, and both of them looked just as bewildered as their parents.

Jessica beamed as she entered, carrying the platter with the roast chicken. "OK." She smiled. "We're all set."

Everyone at the table eyed the food tentatively.

"Go on," Jessica urged. "There's plenty."

"There isn't any seafood in anything?" Elizabeth asked warily.

Everyone at the table laughed, and the optimism that Jessica had been building all afternoon began to diminish.

Alice Wakefield stifled her laughter. "Come on, Liz, that isn't fair. Everything looks beautiful, Jess."

"Thank you," Jessica said coldly.

Elizabeth handed her father the chicken. "Here, Dad, you start."

"Perhaps I should check my will first," Ned Wakefield quipped.

It was just a joke, but it cut through Jessica like a

knife. She had spent all afternoon in the kitchen, trying to make her family see that she had changed, and now they were making stupid jokes. Couldn't they see how much it hurt her?

Everyone at the table ate hesitantly. Jessica sat silently and watched as each person tried a bit of this and a bit of that as if afraid of being poisoned.

Only Elizabeth noticed the cold look on Jessica's face and tried to get her to relax. She began a conversation. "Steve and I were at the mall today. Did you know Ricky is working at Casey's?"

Jessica looked up. "Ricky Capaldo?"

"Yes."

"Since when?" Jessica asked.

Their father looked up. "I'm not surprised."

Both of the twins turned to him. "Why?" Elizabeth asked.

Ned Wakefield looked thoughtful. "Well, normally, I wouldn't discuss something like this, but I'm at my wits' end, and maybe I can get some suggestions." He paused for a moment as if he wanted to choose his words carefully. "You know that Ricky's mother and father got divorced last year?"

"Sure." Jessica nodded. "It was all over school."

"Yes." Her father cleared his throat. "Well, Ricky's grandparents came to me a few weeks ago. It seems Ricky's mom won't let them visit the kids."

66

"She won't let them see their own grandchildren?" Elizabeth asked. "Why?"

"When Ricky's dad left, he left them without much money, and he's stopped paying child support, too." Mr. Wakefield looked around the table. "Ricky's mom is hoping that, maybe, if she keeps his parents from seeing their grandchildren, it will force them to go to their son and pressure him to pay up."

"Poor Ricky." Elizabeth put down her fork. "It must be awful to be in a situation like that."

Jessica turned to her father. "Yeah. Well, maybe it'll work. I mean, Ricky's mom has got to do something."

Their father looked pained. "I know. It's very hard for her. The problem is that Ricky's grandparents have already tried talking to Mr. Capaldo, but he won't listen to reason. There's really nothing more they can do."

"Why doesn't Ricky's mom just sue the father?" Steven asked.

"Well, it's very difficult because he's living in New York now." It was obvious to everyone at the table how concerned Mr. Wakefield was. "The grandparents are such nice people. I feel so bad for them."

"Do you think Ricky's mom can do that?" Elizabeth asked. "Will the court let her cut off the kids' grandparents like that?"

"It's pretty complex," her father answered, "but in cases like this, the court usually sides with the mother. If she doesn't want them to see their grandparents, there isn't much anybody can do about it."

Everyone was quiet for a moment. Jessica was the first to speak. "I don't think the court should be able to do something like that," she said firmly. "I mean, no matter how the mother feels, she shouldn't be allowed to keep the grandparents away."

Ned Wakefield looked down at his plate. "Unfortunately, Jess, I can't explain it to a judge like that."

"I think everybody is sort of missing the point here," Elizabeth said.

It irritated Jessica to see how they listened to Elizabeth with all their attention. *Not like they listen to me*, she thought. Again, the feelings she'd been trying to suppress began to surface.

"The most important thing here isn't the rights of the mother or the rights of the grandparents," Elizabeth went on. "It's the children who are going to suffer. They're the ones who are really losing out."

Ned Wakefield leaned forward. "Go on, Liz."

"Now, not only have the kids lost their father," she continued, "they might lose their grandparents, too—at a time when they probably need all the love they can get."

Her father beamed at her. "That's a wonderful point, Liz. If we can get the judge to see it from that angle, we might have a chance. Look," he went on, "the hearing starts tomorrow. Maybe you'd like to come down and see how it goes."

Elizabeth smiled broadly. "Boy, would I. Maybe I can even get something in *The Sweet Valley News* about it. I've been looking for something to do a series of articles on. This might be it."

"That's a terrific idea," her father agreed.

Everyone at the table began throwing out ideas for the articles. Everyone, that is, but one person.

They were all so busy with plans for the next day that no one noticed when Jessica stood up and quietly left the room.

Six

It wasn't until Jessica had almost gotten to the front of the line that she realized she'd already seen the movie and she hadn't even liked it the first time.

There was nothing else for her to do. She didn't really feel like going to a movie alone, but she didn't want to see anybody either. Not the way she felt.

It doesn't matter what I do, she thought to herself. *I spent all afternoon on that dinner, and they didn't say one word about it. Just those stupid jokes and then all that fuss about that hearing and Elizabeth writing her articles. I'm nothing but a second-class citizen in that family, and that's all I'll ever be.*

Jessica had never felt so totally alone. She thought no one in her family loved or understood her. It was a terrible feeling, and one she couldn't shake no matter how hard she tried.

A few kids she knew were also in line, but fortunately no one was there who she knew well. She didn't want to have to make excuses about why she was at a movie alone. There were only three people in front of her now, and she made a decision. She would just walk for a while. Seeing a bad movie for the second time could only make her feel worse.

Jessica turned from the brightly lit entrance and was walking toward the street when a voice stopped her.

"Hey, Jessica Wakefield!"

Jessica's heart skipped as she looked across the street and saw Nicky Shepard sitting on the hood of his car. As usual, he looked terrific.

Jessica waved and walked over to his car. "Hey, yourself."

"Seeing a movie?" He hopped down from the car hood and shoved his hands into his pockets.

"I was going to"—Jessica tried to think of an excuse—"but I was supposed to meet Lila Fowler, and she couldn't make it."

"So what are you doing now?"

Jessica smiled at Nicky. "I don't know. Got any ideas?"

Nicky returned the smile. "Oh, I don't know. Want to go for a ride?"

Jessica thought for a moment. She liked the idea of spending more time with Nicky. When he had brought her home after Cara's party, he had kissed her several times. The memory of those kisses, warm and tender, was still vivid in Jessica's mind.

She knew Nicky didn't belong to her group, but she was certain that with a little help from her, he'd be able to fit right in. He wasn't like any of the other boys Jessica had dated, but she liked that. Best of all, he seemed to understand her.

Of course, there were a lot of rumors about him, but so far they were just that. Rumors. Nicky had been a real gentleman. It was true he was quiet at school and he didn't have many friends, but Jessica was sure he wasn't involved in drugs in any way.

It's so unfair that people say such mean things behind a person's back, Jessica thought, conveniently forgetting how many times she had been guilty of spreading rumors.

Jessica smiled at Nicky warmly. "I'd love to," she said.

Nicky opened the door for her. Jessica got in, and a moment later Nicky fired the Mustang up, and they took off.

They drove in silence for a bit. Jessica wasn't watching where they were going. She had her eyes on Nicky.

"How come you're so quiet at school?" she finally asked.

Nicky glanced at her and then back at the road. "Oh, I don't really fit in with that scene."

"What scene?"

"You know. That high school scene. Dances and sports and stuff. I've got more important things to do."

"Like what?"

Nicky laughed. "What is this, an interview? I thought your sister was the reporter."

Jessica let the matter drop. "Are we going someplace, or just driving?" Jessica asked.

"I want to show you something," Nicky replied.

He was driving near a park now. It was a small park, the oldest in Sweet Valley, and was used mainly by the people in that neighborhood. Jessica could make out a large, old gazebo with a fancy gingerbread roof.

Nicky pulled up to the curb and parked. He turned the radio up and got out of the car, leaving the door open. Jessica followed him to the gazebo, which stood in the middle of an open space. As she climbed the steps, Jessica looked around her.

It was a beautiful clear night in Sweet Valley. The sky was speckled with stars, and a full moon lit up the park.

Nicky stood with his hands on the railing, looking straight out into the park. He was smiling. He seemed to be deep in thought, as if he were absorbing the darkness that surrounded him.

They stood like that for a long time. Nicky was the first to break the silence.

"Way back when," he said softly, "I don't know, back before we were born, they used to hold dances here. It was part of the original park. That was before the town got built up."

Jessica looked around. The place seemed enchanted. She almost felt that she could hear the laughter of people dancing and having a good time.

"I come here a lot, but I never bring people with me," Nicky said.

"So, how come you brought me?"

"I don't know. You're different from anyone else I know. I didn't want to share this place with just anyone. I wanted to show it to you because I thought . . . I think you're pretty special."

Jessica laughed. "Is that the line you use on the other girls you bring here?"

Nicky looked at her hard. "I said I've never brought anybody else here, and that's the truth."

Jessica suddenly realized she'd hurt him. She could see it in his eyes. It was hard for her to remember that Nicky was very sensitive. He seemed so tough most of the time, and yet, she could see there was something really tender under the surface.

"I'm sorry," Jessica said. She knew what it felt like to be misunderstood by people—what it felt like when people had such a clear idea of what you should be that they didn't even notice what you really were.

"It doesn't matter." Nicky laughed. "Nobody believes what I say half of the time, and they don't care what I say the other half. That's why I'm getting out."

"Getting out?"

He turned to her. "Yeah. I've got a friend in San Francisco. Denny. He's got a good business, and he wants me to come in on it with him. I'm going to take off for there in a few weeks."

Jessica couldn't quite understand what he was saying. "For a vacation?"

"No," Nicky replied. "For good."

"Well, what about school?" Jessica asked.

Nicky let out a little laugh. "I'm through with that Mickey Mouse stuff. Why should I spend my time in a classroom when I could be out in the real world?"

Jessica was shocked. She'd never met anyone who had wanted to quit school. "But—but, what about your parents?"

"They don't care," Nicky said bitterly. "And even if they did, it wouldn't matter. My mind's made up. It'll be for the best anyway. It'll just be easier for them with me gone, with my brother and all. . . ." His voice trailed off.

Jessica felt bad as she looked at Nicky standing in the moonlight. He was like a little boy who thought nobody wanted him.

She turned his face to hers and kissed him softly.

Nicky wrapped his strong arms around Jessica and returned the kiss. They held each other like that for a while with nothing but the sounds of the night and the car radio drifting through the air to them.

Nicky pulled back and looked into Jessica's eyes. The radio began to play a sweet, sad melody.

"Want to dance?" he asked softly. Without waiting for a reply, he took Jessica in his arms and began to move her around the deserted gazebo to the strains of the distant music.

Seven

The shade flew open, flooding Jessica's room with daylight.

Jessica pulled a pillow over her face and moaned into it. "This is not a pleasant way to wake up."

Elizabeth pulled the pillow off her sister's face and sat down beside her. Unlike her twin, Elizabeth had been up and dressed for an hour.

"I'm not surprised you're still asleep," she said, poking her sister playfully. "You didn't get in until after twelve. Where'd you take off to, anyway?"

Jessica turned her face to the wall, and scenes from the evening before came back to her in a rush: the unsuccessful dinner, the chance meeting with Nicky outside the movie theater, the way they danced until midnight, his gentlemanly behavior when he took her home.

Elizabeth interrupted her reverie. "Come on,

Jess. The preliminary hearing starts in an hour and a half, so you'd better get ready."

Jessica rolled back over. "I'm not going to any hearing."

"What?" Elizabeth was surprised. "The visitation hearing with Ricky's grandparents? I thought you were interested."

"I'll read about it in the papers," Jessica muttered.

Elizabeth got up and started to leave the room. But as she got to the door she stopped and whirled around. "OK, Jess. I don't know what's eating you lately, but I, for one, have had just about enough of it. And I think it's pretty rotten of you to let Dad down like this."

"Let Dad down?" Jessica shrieked, now fully awake.

"Yes," Elizabeth answered. "I think he really wants us at that hearing today."

"Wants *you*, Liz," Jessica corrected. "He wants you at the hearing, not us. I think he made that pretty clear last night."

"So that's what it was all about."

Jessica sat up in bed. "What?"

"The mysterious disappearing act you pulled after dinner. You think that just because everyone didn't hang on your every word—"

"Hang on my every word?" Jessica's eyes flashed. "Are you kidding? Nobody ever listens to

80

a thing I say, Liz. They're all too afraid they might miss one of your pearls of wisdom."

Jessica threw her pillow down on the floor and turned her back on her twin.

"Come on, Jess," Elizabeth said, softening her tone. "Dad would love to have you there."

"If he wanted me there, all he had to do was ask me to come," Jessica said bitterly.

"Is that what you want?" Elizabeth asked her sister. "Do you want him to come up here and ask you?"

"I don't want anything, Liz. I don't want to come to the stupid hearing. I don't want Dad to ask me. I don't want anything. I just want to be left alone." Jessica paused for a second. "Anyway, I can't come. I've got a date."

"With whom?"

Jessica picked up her pillow from the floor and got back into bed. She looked smug. "Nicky."

Elizabeth felt as if a wall were being built between her and her twin. "Jess," she said, trying to sound as though she weren't concerned, "you've been seeing a lot of Nicky lately."

"What business is that of yours?" Jessica snapped.

Elizabeth pulled herself together. OK, so Jessica was seeing Nicky Shepard. She had heard rumors about him, but having been hurt by rumors more than once herself, she wasn't eager to put too much faith in them. Still, she knew the kind of people Nicky usually hung around with, a crowd much too fast for Jessica.

Jessica rolled over and faced the wall again. Elizabeth shook her head and left the room. As she walked down to breakfast, she reminded herself that Jessica was a big girl and able to sort things out for herself. Most of the time. Anyway, there really wasn't much she could do about it. If Jessica was going to see Nicky, she was going to see Nicky, and that was that. But Elizabeth decided to talk to her father about Jessica's attitude.

Elizabeth walked into the kitchen just as her father and mother were just finishing their coffee. She set her notebook and purse on the counter.

Ned Wakefield looked up at his daughter. "Good morning. All ready for the first day?"

"Yeah, I guess so." Elizabeth got some cereal, then poured herself a glass of orange juice. She sat across from her mother. "Dad?" she began.

"What?"

"I think maybe you should go upstairs and talk to Jessica."

"Why? What's the problem?"

Elizabeth took a bite of her cereal. "Well, I think we might have hurt her feelings last night. I mean, I think Jess would like to go to the hearing, but she feels as if you don't really care if she's there or not. So maybe if you went up and asked her—"

"Look, Liz," Ned Wakefield interrupted, "I know you have Jessica's best interests at heart, but I don't think your mother and I should have to bow to her every whim. First of all, you two are very different, and I just don't think this is the kind of thing Jessica would be interested in."

"But, Dad, maybe if you just talked to her—"

Her father cut her off again. "No, Liz. We've always tried to raise you two as individuals. Jessica can make up her own mind, and you have to start realizing that. There are lots of times when we do things for Jessica that don't suit you. If Jess wants to come along, fine, but I'm not going to go up and beg her."

Elizabeth looked down at her glass. She debated whether or not to tell them about Nicky, but realized that if she did, she would have to get into Nicky's reputation, which was mostly rumor anyway. Elizabeth decided to drop the whole thing. Eventually Jessica would get over whatever was bugging her.

"Now," her father said after taking the last sip of coffee, "finish up. We're going to have to hustle."

Mrs. Wakefield took her coffee cup and put it in the sink. "Did you talk to the paper about an article?"

"Yes," Elizabeth answered. "I called the features editor yesterday, and he thought it'd be a great idea. He wants me to start today with the preliminary hearing."

"That's a fine idea." Mr. Wakefield picked up his briefcase and motioned toward the door. "All set, star reporter?"

Elizabeth gulped the last of her orange juice, stood up, and grabbed her notebook and purse. "Right!"

She gave her mother a quick kiss and headed out the door after her father. As she walked to the car, Elizabeth decided her father was right about Jessica. This was a big assignment, the biggest the Sweet Valley newspaper had allowed her so far. She was going to have to concentrate all her energies on the hearing. Jessica's problems were just going to have to wait a while.

The preliminary hearing lasted only about an hour. The proceedings were supposed to be informal, but it all looked pretty formal to Elizabeth, who sat off to the side and took notes.

Elizabeth often had to strain to hear what everyone was saying to the judge. They all spoke quietly in the big, wood-paneled courtroom.

Several times Elizabeth studied Ricky, who sat silently between his mother and his younger sister. None of the family members ever looked at one another. It seemed as though they were afraid to make eye contact.

Ricky's grandparents sat at a table next to Mr. Wakefield and Marianna West, one of his partners at the law firm. Elizabeth was immediately struck with compassion for the two old people her father was defending. They spoke with strong Italian accents and often had to have the proceedings explained to them. They looked down at the floor whenever their son, Ricky's father, was mentioned. Mr. Wakefield had told Elizabeth that the grandparents had come to America from Italy. They'd worked hard all their lives to set aside enough money for a comfortable retirement. Now their savings were slowly being eaten away by this legal battle to retain the right to see their grandchildren.

Elizabeth was almost startled by the abrupt way the hearing ended. The judge simply struck his gavel and announced that the court was adjourned. It seemed that nothing had been decided other than that everyone would meet again on Friday for final arguments and a decision by the judge.

Ned Wakefield looked up at Elizabeth and indicated that she should wait for him in the hall. He looked concerned as he began to speak with his clients.

Elizabeth slowly gathered her papers and walked

into the corridor to wait. She went to a nearby water fountain and was about to take a drink when she saw Ricky Capaldo approaching her. "Hi," she said quietly.

Ricky's mouth was set in a dark, hostile expression. "I hear you're doing an article on all of this for the newspaper," he said coldly.

Elizabeth found it hard to look Ricky in the eye. "Yes. Yes, I am."

"Liz, I think I've been a pretty good friend to you, haven't I?"

"Sure, Ricky."

"Then, look." His voice got more forceful than Elizabeth had ever heard it. "I'm asking you not to write this article."

Elizabeth didn't know what to say. "Why—I—" she stammered.

Ricky cut her off. "I know it's a good story for you, but it's my life, and I don't exactly appreciate it's being made public. Please, Elizabeth." Ricky's eyes got a little misty. Without waiting for a reply, he turned around and hurried down the corridor.

Annie Whitman, Ricky's girlfriend, had also come to the preliminary hearing and had sat not far from Elizabeth. While Ricky had been talking to Elizabeth, Annie had been standing off to the side, watching. She looked after Ricky as he ran off but didn't follow him. She knew Ricky needed to be alone.

She walked over to Elizabeth, who was still standing next to the water fountain, trying to catch her breath. Annie pushed a strand of her dark, curly hair away from her face and smiled sympathetically. "Don't be too upset, Liz. Ricky isn't himself lately. This whole thing has been pretty hard on him."

"I guess so," Elizabeth answered.

"He's really angry at his father for leaving. Now his family's got money problems. Ricky's had to take that job at Casey's and everything, just to make ends meet at home."

"I didn't know anything about it until this week."

Annie led Elizabeth to a bench, where they both sat down. "Nobody did. Ricky hardly ever talks about it, even with me. I finally got him to tell me what he felt about the whole thing. That's why I came down here today. He really needs someone."

"How can he let his mother do this?" Elizabeth asked. "Doesn't he care about his grandparents?"

"Ricky loves his grandparents," Annie said sympathetically. "That's why the whole thing is so upsetting. I think he's really bitter toward his father, and he's taking it all out on his grandparents. He won't have anything to do with them, and he's supporting his mother through this hearing." Annie bit her lip as she looked down the hall, where Ricky had disappeared.

Elizabeth said softly, "I think you'd better go find him."

Annie smiled. "You're right." She stood up and walked down the hall.

Elizabeth was touched by how much Annie felt for Ricky. She was there to share his pain and, more importantly, to love him. Elizabeth knew that Ricky needed all the love he could get.

Ned Wakefield's voice brought Elizabeth out of her thoughts. "So, did you get enough stuff for a beginning?"

"I just talked to Ricky." Elizabeth sighed.

Her father exchanged a look with Marianna West, who stood at his side. "Oh? What did he have to say?"

"He doesn't want me to write the article," Elizabeth answered. "He says he doesn't want this whole thing made public. I'm not so sure I don't agree with him." Elizabeth shook her head as she remembered his words. "He just seems so bitter about the whole thing."

Elizabeth's father took her arm and began to lead her down the hall. "So. What are you going to do about the article?" he asked.

"I don't know," Elizabeth answered. "It does seem personal."

"Well, I think with any good story you're going to step on some toes," her father offered. "You just have to ask yourself if the pain you cause some people is greater than the enlightenment you give others."

Elizabeth stopped and smiled at her father. "You know, for an old guy, you can be pretty smart sometimes."

Her father laughed. "Does that solve your problem?"

"No," Elizabeth answered, "but it gives me something to think about."

"Well, I don't know about you two," Marianna West said, smiling. "But all I can think about right now is lunch. How about it? My treat."

Ned Wakefield leaned toward Elizabeth. "I'll give you another piece of advice, my darling daughter. Never turn down a free lunch."

"You're on," Elizabeth said to Marianna West, and the three of them left the courthouse.

Eight

For the fourth time Sheila offered Jessica a beer, and for the fourth time, Jessica declined.

Nicky had picked her up at six o'clock and told her they were going to a party. He didn't tell her the party was going to be in Tierra Verde, about an hour's drive from Sweet Valley. Usually Jessica loved parties, but this one was different. She hardly knew anyone, and the people she did know, she didn't know well. And unlike most of the parties she went to, there was a lot of beer being passed around.

Don't worry, Jessica told herself, *you can handle it*. It was the first time she had been around Nicky's friends, and she was anxious to show him that she could fit in—or rather, that they could find a kind of common ground between their two very different life-styles. That didn't mean that she was going to sit around drinking beer with Nicky's friends, but she was going to try to fit in as much as possible, if only to please Nicky.

The party was being held at the home of a boy named Mike. Jessica hadn't heard his last name. Mike's parents were in Florida for a week, and Mike was taking care of the house. Evidently the party had been going on since they had left. The house was a mess: empty beer cans and pizza boxes littered the basement; the furniture had been moved to one side to make room for dancing; and the driveway in front of the house was a mass of cars and motorcycles. Jessica thought the condition of Mike's house made her bedroom look immaculate in comparison.

She was sitting on a sofa, speaking with two girls she didn't know. Sheila, the one who sat across from her and was doing most of the talking, was a dyed redhead who wore so much mascara and eye liner that she looked like a raccoon. Jessica liked the other girl, who was sitting on the couch beside her. Her name was June. She was petite, with dark, curly hair and very pretty blue eyes. Jessica thought that the reason she liked June was that she had hardly said a word and wasn't a drinker either. She seemed perfectly content to sit there, drinking a Coke and listening to Sheila talk on and on about her boyfriend, Tad.

Nicky hadn't spent much time with Jessica. Soon

after they'd arrived, he had been hustled into a game of pool at the table across the room. But every few minutes, Jessica looked up to find Nicky staring at her. He was smiling sympathetically, a smile that seemed to thank Jessica for putting up with his friends.

Seeing Nicky in this atmosphere only made Jessica feel closer to him. He didn't seem to fit in with these people, either. He didn't talk much and refused the marijuana joint that was being passed around. He had drunk a few beers but didn't seem to be affected by them.

"Don't you think so, Jess?"

Jessica looked at Sheila, who had obviously just asked her a question. "What? I'm sorry, I didn't hear you."

"Boy, are you out of it." Sheila laughed. "I said, just because Tad was dancing with Susan, it doesn't mean that he still likes her, right?"

"Right," Jessica agreed, not having the slightest idea who Susan was or what Sheila was talking about.

"See, June," Sheila turned to the other girl. "That's what I told you. People who went out together once can still be friends. It doesn't mean anything." She reached into the cooler next to her and pulled out another beer. "You want one, Jess?"

Jessica smiled. "No, thanks."

"Here, Jess." June handed Jessica a can of diet Pepsi. "Want one of these?"

Jessica took the can and popped the top open. "Thanks. Where do you go to school, June?"

Before the dark-haired girl could answer, Sheila interrupted. "Oh, she doesn't go to school."

"You don't?" Jessica eyed the girl. She couldn't be more than sixteen.

"No." June seemed a little embarrassed. "I quit last year. I got a job as a waitress."

Jessica decided to drop the subject. "Nicky's a pretty good pool player, isn't he?"

"Oh, yeah," Sheila answered. "But you should see Tad."

Jessica sighed with relief as she noticed the game breaking up. Mike and Nicky walked over to the girls.

"Well," Nicky said, smiling at Jessica, "everyone getting along?"

"Oh, sure." June nodded.

Jessica smiled and tried to look like one of the group. "Sure," she agreed.

Nicky sat on the arm of the couch and put his arm around Jessica. She noticed he was sipping out of a fresh can of beer. He still didn't seem drunk, but Jessica was starting to worry about the drive home.

"We probably should be going pretty soon, Nicky," Jessica said, trying to sound casual.

"Why, the party's just starting," said Mike, sitting down in a chair across from June. He handed her the joint he was smoking.

June accepted the joint and took a quick puff. She didn't seem to enjoy it. Jessica thanked June silently when the girl passed the joint to someone else, and not to Jessica. She hated to draw attention to herself by not accepting, but she was pleased to notice that Nicky refused the joint, too, when it came around to him.

See, she said to herself triumphantly, *all that drug talk was just rumors.*

Just then Tad sauntered over to the group. Jessica could see Sheila brimming with pride as he walked over. Tad was good-looking in a rough sort of way, with longish, straight, black hair and dark, piercing eyes. He sat down on the arm of the chair in which Sheila was sitting. "Did I hear Shepard say something about leaving?" he asked.

"Not him," Mike said. "His girl."

Jessica resisted the urge to tell this baboon that she was nobody's "girl."

"I thought we were going to go all night." Tad's tone seemed to challenge Nicky.

But Nicky didn't seem to notice. "Not me." He smiled at Jessica. "I've got a big day tomorrow."

Jessica breathed a sigh of relief as he got up. She took the hand he offered, and after saying quick goodbyes, the two of them went up the stairs and outside.

It worried Jessica that Nicky was walking a little unsteadily. Maybe the beer had affected him more than she'd thought. She was about to ask him if he thought she should drive when he stopped and leaned against a tree.

"Wait up a second," he said.

Jessica walked over and put her arm around him. "Are you OK?" she asked.

"Sure," he replied. "I just want to take in this beautiful night for a minute."

Jessica rested her head against his chest and looked up at the sky. It *was* a beautiful night. Mike's house was in a wooded section of Tierra Verde. The air was beautifully clear, and, aside from the muffled music from the stereo in the basement, it was quiet.

"I'm sorry," Nicky said quietly.

"About what?"

"You must've been pretty bored in there."

Jessica looked up into his eyes. "I wasn't. Honest."

Nicky smiled as if he could see right through her. "It's nice of you to say that, but I know better. Sometimes I get bored with them, too." He was quiet for a moment. "Listen, I've noticed you've been kind of down tonight. Is it me?"

Jessica reached up and kissed him softly. "Oh,

no, Nicky. Everything's fine with you. Really. It's just—it's just some stuff at home.''

"Like what?" Nicky asked her. "It might make you feel better if you talk about it. Tell me, Jess."

Jessica looked at him. She hadn't really talked to anyone about this, not even Cara. But Nicky seemed so concerned, so caring, that she felt she could open up to him.

She told him everything she was feeling. Everything about how her family treated her at home, how she felt about Elizabeth, her parents, Steven. She found herself telling Nicky things she had never even admitted to herself. How she felt that her parents really didn't want her around and that their lives would be easier without her.

"It's always been me who makes all the trouble," Jessica concluded. "Elizabeth either pays for my mistakes or smooths them over. Sometimes"— Jessica felt tears welling up in her throat as she finished—"I think they wish I'd never been born."

Nicky just held her for a moment as she cried quietly. She could tell from his voice that he understood. "I know you hate to hear people say, 'I know how you're feeling,' but I do, Jess. All my life I've felt like that, too. I know nobody at home would miss me if I weren't around. All my dad wants to do is make money, and my mom needs a lot of time to look after my little brother."

"I'd miss you," Jessica said quietly.

Nicky was silent for a moment. "You wouldn't have to," he said finally.

Jessica pulled back from him slightly. "What?"

"Well." Nicky's mouth was set with determination. "You know I told you about this deal in San Francisco?"

"Yes?"

"Well, I'm going through with it. I called my friend and told him I'd be coming on Friday."

"Friday?" Jessica said. "*This* Friday? The day after tomorrow?"

"Yes," Nicky replied.

"That's so soon."

"Not when you've been thinking about it for years." Nicky took both of Jessica's hands and looked into her eyes. "I wanted to ask you. . . . Look, I want you to come with me."

Jessica was stunned. She almost laughed until she saw how serious Nicky was. "Oh, Nicky . . ."

"Just listen to me for a second. You don't think two people could be more different, right? But why do you think we got together? Maybe it's because we aren't so different, Jess. Maybe we're looking for the same thing. And maybe there's nobody around here who knows how to deal with that. You're different, Jess. You're different from anyone I know. You're just the kind of person I've always been looking for, and I'm not going to let you go."

Jessica stood there silently, letting Nicky's words

wash over her. He was speaking too quickly to give her a chance to think, but in her heart, what he was saying began to make sense.

"You said you've been nothing but trouble for your family, that maybe they'd be better off without you." His words were coming faster now, and he was more excited. "Well, me too. But maybe that's not our fault. Maybe we just weren't meant to be here like this. Maybe somewhere else, on our own, things would be better for everybody."

Everything Jessica had been raised to believe rebelled against what Nicky was telling her. She'd always thought people who ran away from home were losers, people who couldn't make it in the real world. Quitters. But in a way, she was drawn to Nicky's offer. She could see herself coming back to Sweet Valley a few years in the future. She would be independent, sure of herself, someone who had made it on her own without anybody's help. Then her family would see. Then they'd be sorry they had liked Elizabeth.

But even the thought of her twin's name woke something inside Jessica. She and Elizabeth had a bond no one else could understand. They had shared so much. Elizabeth would be hurt if she left, and so would Steven and her parents. Deep inside, in spite of how her family treated her, Jessica was sure they loved her, and she loved them, too.

"Nicky," she began, "I'm very flattered that

you'd ask me, and it doesn't have anything to do with how I feel about you. But—"

Nicky broke away from her. "I knew that 'but' was coming."

"I just couldn't, Nicky." Jessica kissed him softly on the lips. "You understand?"

"Look," Nicky said, "will you just think about it?"

"Nicky . . ."

"Just think about it. That's all."

Jessica looked into his pale-blue eyes. At that moment she thought she really loved him. "OK."

Nicky smiled broadly. "OK. Now I'd better get you home."

Jessica noticed that he was still a little unsteady as he walked to the car. "Are you sure you feel well enough to drive?"

"Of course I do." He seemed a little hurt that she had asked.

Immediately Jessica felt sorry for doubting him. She didn't want Nicky to feel she didn't trust him, but she wasn't sure he should drive in his condition.

Jessica walked to the passenger side and got in. She reached behind her and buckled her seat belt, hoping Nicky wouldn't notice.

Nicky started the car and drove down the driveway, spraying gravel and sand behind him.

Jessica stared ahead in terror. The headlights

lashed through the woods as Nicky gunned the car round curves at breakneck speed.

Although Jessica usually liked riding in a fast car, she asked him to slow down twice. But her requests were met with stony silence. It was as if he didn't even hear her. He just stared straight ahead at the road, breaking his concentration only to flick the ash from his cigarette out the window.

They came to a hill, and in spite of the solid yellow line on the road, Nicky pulled out to pass a slow-moving car. Jessica clenched the edge of the seat in horror as they approached the top of the hill. She couldn't tell whether the glow she saw up ahead was produced by their own headlights or by those of an oncoming car in the same lane.

The Mustang bounced over the top of the incline and was met by two bright headlights and a blaring horn. Jessica screamed as Nicky swerved onto the gravel shoulder. The car swung from left to right, hitting several bumps before flying back onto the road. Nicky said nothing, but the close call must have frightened him. Jessica breathed a sigh of relief as he eased off the gas pedal and slowed to a more reasonable speed.

They were entering the outskirts of Sweet Valley now, and the road was more familiar. Nicky leaned over the wheel to light another cigarette. He didn't even notice the stop sign that became a blur as they sped into the intersection. Just then Jessica saw a

101

blue convertible coming at them from her side. She braced herself for the crash. Instinctively, Nicky slammed on the brakes and cut the wheel hard to the left. The Mustang spun a full one hundred and eighty degrees, missing the blue car by inches. Nicky fought to stay on the road, but it was too much for him. The car spun off the shoulder and the rear slammed into a telephone pole before it shuddered to a stop.

Jessica opened her eyes. She realized slowly that she was unhurt. The crash hadn't been that bad. She turned to Nicky, who seemed a little shaken. Without saying a word, he jumped out of the car and walked around to check the damage.

Jessica unbuckled her seat belt and got out of the car. Nicky was kneeling by the crushed rear fender.

"How bad is it?" she called to him.

"Only the fender's bent," he answered, "but I can't pull it away from the tire."

Jessica noticed for the first time the cut above Nicky's eye. "Are you OK?" she said as she approached him.

Nicky got to his feet and touched the cut. "Yeah. It's just a scratch. I must've hit the steering wheel when we caught that pole."

"The other car didn't even stop."

"Lucky for us." Nicky kicked the dented fender. "All we need now is cops."

Jessica looked around. They were still some distance from town, but there was a gas station just ahead of them.

"What do we do now?" she asked.

Nicky kicked the car again and sighed. "Call my folks, I guess."

Nicky went back to the car and pulled out his jacket. He walked around to Jessica and threw it over her shoulders.

"You OK?" he asked her.

Jessica couldn't look at him. "Yeah. I'm fine," she muttered.

He put his arm around her, and they walked to the gas station.

Jessica sat in the backseat of the Shepards' car and waited for Nicky to open the door. The ride back to her house had been absolutely silent, which Jessica welcomed after all the yelling that had gone on at the crash site.

Nicky's father bore a strong resemblance to his son and seemed to be just as stubborn and quick-tempered. He never even gave Nicky a chance to say anything before he launched into a tirade. Most of it concerned the car and how much it was going to cost to get it fixed. Mr. Shepard never asked once if Jessica and Nicky were hurt. Nicky's mother said almost nothing. She just looked at her son, thin lines of disappointment edging her mouth.

Just before the tow truck arrived, Nicky's father turned to his son, his face white with anger. "This is the last straw, Nicky," he said harshly. "I don't know what you're trying to prove with this lifestyle you lead, but I know what you're accomplishing. You're ruining us financially and causing your mother and me nothing but pain."

Nicky looked at his father. His voice had the same loveless tone. "Don't worry. I'll be out of your hair soon enough. I'm taking off."

"Good," his father snapped back. "Maybe living on your own will teach you some responsibility. God knows we haven't been able to!"

That was the last thing they had said to each other, and now, as Jessica was waiting to get out of the car, she had no idea what she was going to say to the Shepards.

Nicky opened the door, got out, then helped Jessica out. She took one last look at Nicky's parents, decided against saying it had been nice meeting them, and walked away without a word.

Nicky went with her up to the door. "I'm sorry about all that. I should've let you drive. We wouldn't have been in a mess like this."

"Oh, I don't know," Jessica said, trying to lighten the moment. "You've never seen me drive."

Her joke got a smile out of Nicky. He leaned over

and kissed her lightly. "Thanks. Promise you'll think about my offer?"

Jessica had already put the idea of going to San Francisco out of her mind, but she didn't want to tell Nicky just then. "OK, I promise," she said.

He smiled at her and walked back to his parents' car.

Inside, Jessica was relieved to find that everyone had gone to bed. She didn't feel like talking to anyone at the moment.

She turned off the hall light and walked upstairs to her room. She got ready for bed, but it was a long time before she could get to sleep. The events of the day kept going through her mind in a mad whirl.

As she was lying in bed, the thought suddenly came to her of how close she had been to a disaster. Not just the car accident. What would have happened if Nicky's parents had decided to tell her parents about the crash? She could just imagine her father and mother being dragged from their sleep to be told that Jessica had been in a car accident because her date was drunk.

They would have forbidden her to see Nicky. They couldn't understand him, not the way she did. Jessica could see so much of herself in Nicky, and in many ways, she really felt she loved him.

Suddenly her mind was filled with a romantic notion of the two of them in San Francisco. They would have a beautiful little apartment that overlooked the bay. They would have interesting friends, and Nicky would be a successful business-man, and after a while . . .

Whoa, girl, Jessica thought, pulling herself back to reality. *No matter how you feel about Nicky, you can't run out on your family. How would they feel if you ran away? And all of your friends. Lila, Cara . . . how would it be never to be able to see them again?*

Of course, Jessica couldn't resist thinking, *they could come to visit on weekends. . . .*

Jessica shook her head and rolled over. She had to stop thinking like this.

Tomorrow, I am going to fix up this whole thing, she resolved. *I'll talk to Mom and Dad and Liz and Steve. We'll get everything out in the open, and soon, after they realize how wrong they've been about me, everything will be different. Tomorrow,* she added as she drifted off to sleep, *everything changes.*

Nine

"Mom, Dad, I want you to know I'm tired of the way things have been around here. I know I've been the cause of a lot of trouble, and I'm willing to try hard to be a better person. But you've got to help me. You have to stop thinking of me as the old Jessica and give me a chance to change."

Jessica looked into the mirror as if she expected a response. She had gotten up early to work on the speech, and this was the best version by far. She took a deep breath, then headed toward the door. Her parents were downstairs having breakfast, and she wanted to get this whole thing over with as soon as possible.

Maybe I should run it by Liz, she thought to herself as she passed her sister's room. She tightened her robe slightly and opened Elizabeth's door a crack.

It was still very early, and her twin was in bed,

sound asleep. Jessica stepped in and stared at her. Many things ran through her mind.

She thought about all the things she and Elizabeth had been through—all the history they had shared. She remembered how she felt the time when Elizabeth lay in a coma and none of them knew if she was going to be all right. And how awful it had been when Elizabeth had been kidnapped.

Jessica had to fight to hold back her tears as she realized that she had been responsible for both of those near tragedies. In fact, she had been responsible for almost every bad situation her twin had gotten into. Yet, somehow, Elizabeth had always managed to make it right.

Jessica closed the door silently. She couldn't bring herself to talk to Elizabeth about all this. Not yet. Maybe after she had smoothed everything over with her mother and father—maybe then. Right now, it was just too painful.

Downstairs, Ned and Alice Wakefield sat across from each other at the breakfast table. They were sipping coffee and talking as Jessica entered the room.

"Well," her father said, "you're up early."

Jessica smiled. "Good morning," she said brightly.

Her mother got up and put her coffee cup in the sink. Jessica smiled at how pretty she looked in the tailored gray suit she wore. "Just in time to see me off," Mrs. Wakefield said.

"You have to leave so early?" Jessica couldn't keep the disappointment out of her voice. She'd really wanted to talk to both her parents.

"Yes," her mother said. "I've got an early meeting, and I can't be late."

Jessica forced a smile. "Sure," she said. She returned her mother's hug and watched as Mrs. Wakefield kissed her husband and breezed out of the room.

Well, Jessica thought to herself, *I'll just have to start with Dad. I'll talk to Mom later.*

Jessica put a tea bag in a mug and filled it with hot water. She sat down where her mother had been sitting, opposite her father. "How's the hearing going?"

Her father was reading a section of the newspaper and didn't look up from it. "Oh. Not too well. I'm afraid that in a case like this, there isn't much we can do. The law keeps visitation rights and alimony payments separate, so we haven't got much to stand on."

"Dad," Jessica began, "I want you to know—"

Mr. Wakefield continued. "The funny part about that is that the law tries to protect the kids, but it isn't working in this case. It's just giving the mother the right to decide who the kids see and who they don't."

Jessica began again. "I want you to know I'm tired—"

"You know, your sister is right. I think if we could just get the court to see that the kids are losing out, that they need their grandparents' love, we could win."

Ned Wakefield was so wrapped up in his court case that he didn't see the disappointed look on Jessica's face.

"What were you saying, honey?" he said distractedly.

"Liz is doing a pretty good job on the article?"

Again he didn't notice the flat tone of her voice. "She sure is. I'm really glad she had the courage of her convictions and decided to go ahead with the story. She's going to make a great reporter someday."

But what about me, Dad? Jessica thought to herself. *What about me?*

Her father checked his watch and swallowed the last of his coffee. "Speaking of running off . . . I've got to go." He jumped up and gave Jessica a quick kiss on the cheek. "See you later, honey."

Then, for the first time that morning, he noticed the look on his daughter's face. The conversation concerning Jessica came back to him.

"Is something wrong, Jess?" he asked.

Jessica fought hard to keep back the tears. "No, nothing's wrong."

110

"Look." He set down his briefcase and sat on the chair next to her. "If you want to, you know you're welcome to come along on Friday and watch the hearing too. I don't know how interesting it would be for you, though."

"Does Liz find it interesting?"

"Well, yes, but you and your sister are different."

Jessica didn't reply.

"Well, I just wanted you to know you're welcome to tag along," Mr. Wakefield finished.

Jessica didn't look up at him as he kissed her again. "Thanks," she muttered.

He smiled at her and walked out of the kitchen.

Jessica sat at the table and swirled the tea bag around in the cup until the tea was too cold to drink. She tried to tell herself that both her parents had very busy schedules and if she had let them know how serious all of this was, they would have stayed. She said it to herself a million times, but it didn't make her feel any better. She still had this gnawing feeling that if she had been Elizabeth, they would have had more time to listen.

She thought about the last-minute offer her father had made to let her "tag along" at the hearing. Jessica was willing to bet money that Elizabeth had put him up to that. Who were they trying to kid? she thought. If he had wanted her to go, he would have asked her in the first place. And he wouldn't have called it "tagging along," as if her going to the trial was just an afterthought.

Jessica was jerked from her thoughts by Steven's entering the kitchen. He was wearing an old warm-up suit and had a towel wrapped around his neck. He was obviously planning to go running.

"Good morning," he said to Jessica as he poured himself some orange juice.

Well, Jessica thought, *I may as well try talking to Steve. After all, he and I haven't been on perfect terms lately. Maybe it's time for us to make up.*

"Steve," Jessica began, "can I talk to you?"

Steven downed the orange juice in one gulp and checked his watch. "Look, Jess, can it wait? I want to get in some jogging right now. I'm playing tennis later with some guys, and I need to loosen up."

"You have to go this second?" Jessica asked, disappointed.

"Sorry," Steven called from the door. "We'll talk when I get back. Promise."

Jessica's heart sank. Steven was too busy jogging to talk to her. Didn't he realize how serious all of this was?

Jessica's thoughts were interrupted by the telephone ringing. She stomped over and picked up the kitchen extension.

"Hello," she said listlessly.

"Well, somebody got up on the wrong side of the bed."

Jessica recognized Lila Fowler's voice. "Oh, hi, Lila."

"Is this really Jessica Wakefield?" Lila spoke in a mocking tone. "I thought maybe you had died or left town or something."

If you only knew, Jessica thought. "No, I'm sorry I haven't called. I've just been—busy."

"I talked to Cara, and she said she hadn't heard from you in a while either. What's up? You getting a new circle of friends?"

Jessica knew that last comment was a stab at Nicky, but she let it go. "No. Like I told you, Lila, I've been busy."

"Oh, well, excuse me," Lila said indignantly. "I just called to see if you wanted to go shopping today."

"Today—uh—" About the last thing Jessica wanted to do was spend the whole day shopping with Lila. "No, Lila, I can't today. I'm spending some time with my father," she lied.

"Oh, OK." There was a slight pause. "Jess, are you OK?" Lila asked.

"Sure. Why?"

"I don't know. You sound funny."

"Well, you know me, Lila. I'm a funny girl." Jessica tried to be cheerful, but her heart wasn't in it.

"Yeah. Well, give me a call later if you want to."

"Sure," replied Jessica. "I will."

113

They said goodbye, and Jessica hung up the phone. Jessica knew that for some reason she was pulling away from her friends. She couldn't figure it out, but now they all seemed childish. Maybe Nicky really was having an effect on her.

And maybe it isn't half bad, she added to herself.

Just then Jessica heard Elizabeth bustling around. Well, she would give it one last try. If anybody was willing to listen to her, Elizabeth was. Her twin had always been the closest person to her, and she seemed to know just what Jessica was thinking. Somehow, the two of them would be able to work this whole thing out.

Jessica took one sip of her tea, now cold and bitter, and tossed the rest of it in the sink. She rinsed off the other breakfast dishes, then went upstairs. Elizabeth was in the bathroom putting on the final touches of her makeup.

"Jess, do me a favor." It was obvious that Elizabeth was in a hurry. "Loan me that new lipstick of yours. I haven't got one that's right, and I want to look perfect today."

Jessica nodded and went into her room to get the lipstick. She found it right where she'd left it, under a stack of magazines.

"Here," she said as she reentered the bathroom. She walked over to the dressing table and handed her twin the tube.

"Thanks." Elizabeth smiled. She took a brush off

114

the table and carefully outlined her lips. When she had finished using the lipstick, she asked, "Does this outfit look too casual?"

"Stand up and turn around," Jessica commanded. She looked Elizabeth over. She was wearing a blue cotton skirt with a matching jacket over a white silk blouse. Jessica thought the outfit was conservative but perfect for Elizabeth. "You look fine," she said.

"Thanks. I've got a meeting at the *News* this morning. I have to show my editor my preliminary notes and talk about the direction I'm taking with the article." She was talking quickly, and she hurried into her room.

Jessica followed her sister, watching her carefully. Elizabeth hadn't even noticed that Jessica had followed her into her room. She was too wrapped up in her own thoughts, the hearing, the articles. All of these things were so important to Elizabeth, so important that they had blinded her to what was going on between them.

"Liz," Jessica began, "we have to talk."

Elizabeth looked up at her twin. "Sure, Jess." She checked her watch. "What's up?"

Oh, Liz, Jessica thought, *it all would have been OK if you hadn't done that. If you just hadn't looked at your watch.*

"What is it?" Elizabeth repeated. She had

noticed a dark look come over Jessica's face. "Is it Nicky?"

"No, Nicky's great," Jessica replied. She forced her voice to become more casual. "We can talk later. I'm sure you're in a hurry."

"Well, I'm supposed to be down there at nine o'clock, which only gives me twenty minutes," she said hesitantly. "But if it's important, Jess, I can skip the whole thing."

"No, it's nothing," Jessica said. *I don't want to be any more trouble for you*, she added to herself.

"OK, if you say so." Elizabeth picked up her note pad and folders and gave her twin a hug. "We'll talk later. When I get home."

"Sure."

Elizabeth started out the door. "Oh, here." She ran back into the bathroom and picked up the lipstick. "Thanks again, Jess. Wish me luck."

"Good luck," Jessica said softly as her twin breezed past her.

Jessica stood there and listened as Elizabeth shut the front door. She heard the Fiat roar to life, and then listened to the sound as it disappeared down their street.

The house was quiet now. Jessica wandered into her bedroom, lost in her depression.

Everything Nicky had said came back to her, and worse: it was all true. She didn't belong in the family. The only one with any problems and the cause

116

of everyone else's. The only one with nothing to do. As Nicky had said, she just didn't fit in.

Suddenly Jessica felt she had to talk to Nicky. He was the only one who really understood her. The only one who cared for her. They were alone together. Just the two of them.

A chill swept through Jessica as she realized what she was admitting to herself. She picked up the phone and dialed Nicky's number. The phone rang several times before it was picked up.

"Hello?" It was a young boy's voice. Jessica knew it must be Nicky's little brother.

"Hello. May I speak to Nicky, please?"

"Just a second."

Jessica heard the phone clattering down and the boy yelling for Nicky in the background. After a couple of minutes, the phone was picked up again.

"Yeah?" It was Nicky's voice.

"Hi, it's Jessica." Just the sound of his voice made her feel better, convinced her that she was doing the right thing.

"Hi," he said softly. "I was just going to call you."

"You were?"

"Yeah. Listen, I'm leaving tonight."

"Tonight?" Jessica panicked. "I thought you weren't going until Friday!"

"Things have gotten really bad around here after last night. I've got to get out now."

Jessica didn't know how to reply.

After a short silence, Nicky spoke again. "Have you been thinking about my offer?"

Jessica took a deep breath. "Actually, that's what I called to talk to you about."

Ten

Jessica hardly slept a wink Thursday night. It all still seemed like a dream, although she knew it wasn't. She awoke on Friday morning knowing that Nicky was already in San Francisco, waiting for her. By nighttime, she would be there with him, with someone who understood and cared about her. She and Nicky would be starting a new life, together.

Monday would probably be the day when everyone at school found out. Lying in bed, Jessica smiled as she imagined the news running through the halls. What a story! Jessica Wakefield had left Sweet Valley! Of course, no one would know where she was. She had talked to Lila and Cara the previous night but had resisted the urge to tell them anything. She couldn't. She decided that she might write Cara a letter after a while, just to tell her she was all right. Of all her friends, Cara would be most upset, Jessica decided. Lila might even be happy to have less competition.

Of course, Jessica reflected, her family would be upset for a while, but they would get over it. They'd try to find her at first, but then her father would get caught up again in his law practice, her mother with her design clients, and everyone, of course, would be busy helping Steven put his life back together.

And Elizabeth. Elizabeth would be OK too. She'd grow up to become a star reporter on some fancy newspaper somewhere, and she'd forget about what's-her-name, the twin she used to have.

Jessica planned to tell her parents she was spending the weekend at Lila's. They were all so wrapped up in the hearing that no one would even notice she was missing until Sunday.

Sunday. Jessica thought about Sunday at the Wakefields'. Sleeping in late and waking up to a leisurely brunch and then a trip to the beach with friends.

No, she thought. She had to put things like that out of her mind. It wasn't going to be like that anymore. She would wait until her family had left for the day, and then she'd pack her things and head for the bus station.

Jessica had piled up some of her clothing and belongings in stacks in the closet. It wouldn't take her longer than a couple of hours to get everything into suitcases. She would take the local bus and get off at the station, leaving the Fiat for Elizabeth. Everything would be better because she'd finally be out of their lives. That was what they wanted, wasn't it?

Suddenly it occurred to Jessica her family might not believe she had run away. Maybe they would think she'd been kidnapped. Jessica remembered the pain her parents had gone through when Elizabeth had been kidnapped by a lunatic orderly at the Joshua Fowler Memorial Hospital. She couldn't put her parents through that again.

What could she do? Maybe she could tell Cara, and Cara could reassure her family later. No, that was no good. Cara couldn't keep any kind of secret; she'd be at the bus station with Jessica's family and the Sweet Valley High School Band before Jessica had even packed. Telling someone in her family was out, and a phone call wasn't a good idea. They might be able to trace it to where she was, or maybe they would try to talk her into coming home.

No, the only choice was a note. Yes, that was it. She would leave a note that they could find after she'd gone. She could convince them that this was for the best, and maybe they'd understand. Maybe they'd come to see it all as she had.

Jessica began to compose the note in her head and instantly regretted not having paid more attention in the creative-writing class she had taken the previous year.

What should she write? She didn't want to make anybody feel bad, or did she? Well, maybe just a little, she thought. After all, it wasn't her fault that she was being forced to run away. Maybe, she thought, she'd make her family feel a little guilty, but she'd also try to convince them that this was all for the best and that she'd be better off on her own.

Jessica threw the sheets back and got out of bed. She put on her robe and sat down at her desk. She was thinking about what she'd write as she pulled a piece of stationery out of her drawer. It was pretty lavender paper that Elizabeth had given her for her last birthday.

No, no, she wasn't going to think about her birthday! That would just make her feel sad, and she didn't want to feel sad. She didn't want to think about anything that might make her change her mind.

Jessica's first problem was deciding to whom she should address her letter. The entire family was too general. She didn't want to single out her mother or her father either. If she picked just one, it would make the other feel left out.

The only choice was Elizabeth. Besides, Elizabeth was the only one who could read her bad handwriting.

She wrote:

Dear Liz,

By the time you get this, I will be far away. I'm sorry if my leaving causes you all a lot of pain, but it will be better for all of us in the long run. There are many reasons why I'm going. It isn't just your fault. You can't help being the way you are any more than I can. You're so good. It would just be better for all of you if you'd forget that I ever even existed. I've never been anything but trouble anyway. This doesn't mean I'm forgetting about you. I'll be thinking a lot about all of you as I take the bus to my new home. I love you, Liz. And make sure you tell Mom and Dad that I love them too, and Steve, even though I know he hates me. Someday I'll return, I promise, but not for a long time. Please don't try to find me. My mind is made up. I'm sorry for all the trouble I've caused.

Still your loving sister,
Jessica

Jessica put down the pen and wiped the tears

from her eyes. She read the note over. Suddenly a thought came to her, and she added at the bottom:

P.S. I'm leaving you my new jeans. I think they make me look fat anyway.

Jessica carefully folded the note and put it in a matching envelope. She smoothed it out until it lay perfectly flat.

There was a knock at her door, and Elizabeth flew in. Jessica quickly slid the note into a book.

"Jess, help," Elizabeth said in desperation. "I'm late, and I need to borrow your green scarf."

Jessica looked at her twin. Elizabeth was dressed like the perfect reporter in a smartly tailored tan suit. Jessica pulled the scarf out of her drawer and walked over to Elizabeth. She tied it around her sister's neck and stepped back.

"How do I look?" Elizabeth asked, smiling.

Jessica fought hard to hold back the tears. She crossed to her twin, wrapped her arms around her, and hugged her with all her might. "Beautiful. Just beautiful."

"Hey." Elizabeth pulled back and noticed that Jessica was crying. "I knew I looked good today, but I didn't think it was anything that deserved tears. What's wrong?"

"Nothing." Jessica wiped her tears away with the back of her hand and turned so she wasn't facing her sister. She pretended to be busy with something on her dresser. "I'm being silly. I'm just so proud of you, Liz."

Elizabeth said nothing for a second. She could tell when Jessica was making excuses. She knew her twin too well to be fooled.

"Hey. What's up?"

Jessica turned and faced her twin. She forced a smile. "Nothing, really. I'm fine. I'm just feeling sort of— I don't know—*funny* today."

"Yeah. You look real funny."

"Thanks a lot."

Ned Wakefield's voice drifted up from downstairs. "Hey, Hemingway, let's get a move on."

"I've got to go." Elizabeth looked at her sister with concern.

"I know. It's OK. I'm fine, really."

The twins exchanged a look, and Jessica almost spilled the whole plan. She wanted to. She wanted to tell her sister the whole thing and have Elizabeth convince her to stay. But then, the moment was gone, and she couldn't.

"I'll be back this afternoon, and then we'll talk. OK?"

Jessica smiled at her. "No, I'm spending the weekend at Lila's. But I'll see you Sunday." She almost choked on the words.

Elizabeth returned the smile and hugged her sister again. "Sure. Have a good time. I'll call you and let you know how the hearing comes out."

"Good. Tell Dad good luck for me. OK?"

Elizabeth nodded and walked out the door. Jessica listened to the sounds of everyone leaving, and then she was alone again.

She walked over to her desk and pulled her letter out of the book. Carefully and with great affection she wrote her sister's name on the envelope.

Deep down, Jessica knew the real reason for writing the letter. She wanted her family to come and find her. She didn't really want to leave. That was why she had included the reference to the bus in her note. Most likely, Elizabeth would come home, find the letter, figure out where Jessica had gone, rush to the bus station, and beg her sister to stay. Everything would be different then. Then they'd all take her seriously.

She propped the letter on her dresser and began to pack. It took her longer than she'd expected, and when she was done, just after noon, her room was so clean, she hardly recognized it. Nothing was out of place.

Jessica picked up her two suitcases and carried them to the door. As she looked back into her room, she was suddenly flooded with memories. So many of the things that had happened in the room with the chocolate-brown walls came back to her in such vivid detail that she felt she couldn't take it anymore. She slammed the door and headed for the local bus.

What Jessica didn't know was that in slamming the door, she had created a breeze in the room. Not a big wind, but just enough to knock the letter over and cause it to fall behind her dresser.

Eleven

Elizabeth scanned the faces in the courtroom. Ricky, his mother, sister, and grandparents all just stared at the floor most of the time. The grandparents didn't seem to be able to follow the proceedings. Often during the hearing Ned Wakefield or Marianna West had to lean over and explain to them what was going on. But Elizabeth could tell that they understood the importance of the hearing. They looked as though they had taken extra time with their appearance. That made her a little sad, thinking that they had put on their best clothes, maybe even bought new ones, for an occasion as sad as this one was.

The look on Ricky's face upset Elizabeth. At school Ricky had always been cheerful. It was strange and disturbing to see him like this. He never smiled once during the proceedings, not even when he was speaking with Annie, who sat in the row behind Ricky's family, wearing a sad expression and watching closely.

Ned Wakefield and Marianna West took notes and exchanged them frequently. Elizabeth could tell by the looks on their faces that it wasn't going well. They presented their arguments effectively, but their case was weak. All the testimony boiled down to one point: neither Ricky nor his sister nor his mother seemed to want contact with the two old people, and the court had to respect Mrs. Capaldo's wishes.

Elizabeth spent most of her time at the final hearing taking notes and watching carefully. There was a lot to absorb, so many terms that she didn't understand and would have to ask her father about later.

The defense counsel was a man named Murray Long. Elizabeth had talked to him briefly before the session, and he seemed to be a nice man. He too shared the pain of Ricky's grandparents, but he had a job to do, and he was doing it to the best of his ability. In his final arguments Mr. Long stated that the alimony payments were not the important issue of the hearing. What was at stake was the mother's right to decide who should have contact with her children. If it was her wish that the grandparents be prohibited from visiting the children, there wasn't much the court could do about it. He spoke quietly and with determination.

Mr. Long finished his comments and sat down. The judge nodded to Mr. Wakefield, who stood to give his argument.

"Your Honor," Ned Wakefield began, "we have a very complex problem here. It seems to me to be a case of the law versus justice." He paused for a moment and then went on. "In all of this, we have discussed in great detail a lot of fine points of the law, but none of us has mentioned the point that is at the bottom of the whole problem. This is a case that should never have been brought to court in the first place. The bottom line here, it seems to me, is that children need love. They need it as much as they need food or air or education. They need it to grow and to develop into responsible, caring adults. There is no doubt that many people have suffered in this case. Mrs. Capaldo has certainly suffered. She has been forced to become the sole support of her family. But my clients have also suffered. They have spent a great deal of time and money, and why? Because they want to give these children the love they so desperately need." Mr. Wakefield paused.

From her vantage point, Elizabeth noticed that Ricky had begun to move uncomfortably in his chair. Then, like a spring, he shot up from the chair and marched out of the courtroom. Annie began to get up, but Elizabeth stopped her with a look. After putting her notebook down on the seat next to her, Elizabeth followed Ricky into the corridor.

She came out of the double doors and saw him sitting on a bench in front of the elevators, his head in his hands. Elizabeth walked quietly to the bench and sat down beside him.

She said nothing at first. After a moment Ricky looked up and saw her there. He made no sign of recognition, and Elizabeth could see that he was crying.

"Getting a lot of good material for your article?" he snapped bitterly.

Elizabeth bit her lip. "Look, Ricky. I don't think you really feel—"

He cut her off in anger. "How do you know how I feel? You can't imagine how I feel. Everything is so perfect for you." His voice got a little quieter. "You know what it's like? One day everything is great: you've got a mother and a father and a family; and the next day, they're telling you everything has changed. They can't get along anymore. They can't live together anymore. But nobody asks you. Nobody asks you how you feel. I love my father, and I love my mother, but my father took off, and now, it's pretty clear to me that he doesn't want anything to do with us. Fine. Well, I don't want anything to do with him either. Him or his parents." Ricky burst into sobs.

Elizabeth didn't know what to say. Ricky was right. She had no idea what it would be like to have her family torn apart like this.

She put her hand on Ricky's arm tenderly and tried to find the right words. "Ricky. I know I can't imagine what it must be like for you. But think about your grandparents. It must be terrible for them, too. Why do you think they're doing this? They're only doing it because they love you. They just want to be there for you."

"I don't care why they're doing this!" Ricky burst out. "I don't care. I just want them to leave us alone! And I want you to leave me alone, too!"

Elizabeth was stunned for a moment. She tried to control her anger, but she couldn't. "OK. Fine. You know, Ricky, I always thought you were such a strong person, but I guess I was wrong. I watched you when you helped Annie through her problems. I watched you sit by her hospital bed and beg her not to give up. I never once thought I would see you giving up."

"I'm not giving up anything!"

"Don't give me that. You're mad at your father, and you want to get back at him, so this is how you're doing it. By hurting your grandparents, who never did anything to you other than love you. Well, if that's how you feel, then you're doing the right thing by turning away from your grandparents. Because you don't deserve that love,

Ricky. Go ahead. Give up. Just put it out of your mind and get more and more bitter. That's really smart."

Elizabeth choked up. She knew she had a lot more to say, but she also knew none of it would make any difference now. She got up and walked back into the courtroom.

Her father was just finishing his statement.

"I know the courts can't tell people whom they should love and whom they shouldn't. But it seems to me, if we help to open the door here, a lot of people are going to be happier in the future. Please, Your Honor." He paused. "Think of the children. The children," he repeated quietly. "That's what is really at stake here. Think of them."

Mr. Wakefield sat down slowly. Elizabeth noticed that Ricky had reentered the courtroom and was now standing at the back, by the doors.

Everyone began to shift uncomfortably in his seat. Judge Winters sat still for a long moment. Once it looked as though he was going to leave the courtroom; then, he seemed to decide against it.

"Normally," he began, "I would retire at this point to consider all the testimony and make a decision. But in this case I'm afraid that the decision has already been made for me."

Elizabeth watched as Ricky's grandparents looked hopefully at her father. Ned Wakefield just stared down at the papers in front of him, not offering them any encouragement.

Judge Winters continued, "The law is quite clear as to the wishes of a parent or guardian and in a case such as this one—"

"Excuse me, Judge Winters." The whole courtroom turned and watched as Ricky walked up the aisle. "I would like to say something, if it isn't too late."

The judge glanced at both tables of lawyers. There seemed to be no objection from either side.

"Yes?" Judge Winters motioned for Ricky to come forward.

Ricky walked to the front of the courtroom. He cleared his throat and began. "You see, I haven't said anything throughout this whole deal, but I've been thinking it over. . . ." He paused and turned to his mother. "Mom, this isn't right. What we're trying to do here is punish Dad for leaving, and it isn't fair. It isn't fair to Grandma and Grandpa, and it isn't fair to Toni and me."

Ricky's little sister, Toni, shifted her gaze from Ricky to her mother and back again.

Ricky looked embarrassed. "And it isn't fair to you either, Mom," he added.

No one said anything. Ricky looked around the courtroom. When he caught Elizabeth's eye, he smiled.

"That's all I wanted to say," he finished. He nodded to the judge and returned to his seat.

Judge Winters cleared his throat. He looked hopefully at Mrs. Capaldo, and then he stood up. "May I see all of the litigants in my chambers without their counsel?"

The judge picked up his papers and walked out of the courtroom. Ricky, Toni, his mother, and grandparents followed.

Elizabeth walked up to the row behind her father and leaned toward him. "What do you think is happening?"

Ned Wakefield turned and smiled. "I think everything is going to be OK. Don't quote me, but I think that article of yours is going to have a happy ending."

Elizabeth returned her father's smile. She sat back to wait for the judge to return. It seemed like forever. They were out a full hour. When they returned, Ricky walked between his grandmother and his mother, and his grandfather held little Toni by the hand. They were all smiling, but their eyes showed that some tears had been shed.

They returned to their places at the tables, and the judge looked over the courtroom. He was obviously pleased. "I am very happy to say, it won't be necessary for me to make a decision in this case," he said. "The two parties have reached an agreement in my chambers."

Ricky turned and gave Elizabeth a smile. The judge dismissed the case, and all parties shook hands. Ricky and Annie immediately made their way to Elizabeth.

"Boy," Ricky said, "I don't know what to say, Liz."

Elizabeth smiled at him. "You don't have to say anything."

Ricky smiled at her again and tightened his grip on Annie's arm. Then the two of them walked away and joined his family.

Ned Wakefield approached his daughter. He was beaming with pride. "Something tells me you had a hand in all this."

"Could be." Elizabeth smiled. "Sometimes people just need a little push."

Her father wrapped an arm around her and led her out into the hall. "Well, whatever it was, I appreciate it, and I'm sure the Capaldos do, too."

Elizabeth looked down the hall at the group of people hugging and smiling. She felt warm and wonderful, and she knew that everything was going to be all right for them, even without their father.

Marianna West walked up to Elizabeth and her father. "It's two-thirty. Anybody for a late lunch?"

"Sure," Elizabeth's father agreed. "Alice went to a site this morning, but she said she'd be working at home this afternoon, and we can see if Steve wants to join us. After all, this is a celebration."

"Sounds great," Marianna West said, smiling. "Why don't we meet at the Palomar House?"

"Count me out." Elizabeth was looking through the notes she'd accumulated during the trial. "I've got to put some of this on paper while it's still fresh in my mind. Besides, I'd like to give Jess a call at Lila's."

"Anything wrong?" her father asked.

"No," Elizabeth replied. "I don't think so."

"OK, I'll give you a lift," her father said as they walked out of the courthouse.

The happy ending of the afternoon was somehow spoiled when Elizabeth thought of her sister and how strangely she'd acted that morning. Well, Elizabeth was on her way home now and could call her sister. One way or another, she was determined to get to the bottom of all this stuff with Jessica.

Twelve

Elizabeth decided to start her article before calling Jessica. She'd have the whole house to herself for a while, since Steven had agreed to go to lunch with her parents and Marianna West.

She thought about how much better Steven seemed lately. He'd been out to play tennis with some friends that morning, and now she heard him singing to himself as he finished getting dressed for lunch. All in all, it looked as if they were getting the old Steven Wakefield back.

"Better get a move on," Elizabeth shouted to him. "Mom and Dad are waiting in the car."

"I'll be done in a second," Steven called back.

Elizabeth took off the scarf she'd borrowed from her sister and set it on her dresser. *No*, she thought to herself as she glanced at it. *I'm always bugging Jess about not returning things. Maybe I'd better practice what I preach.*

Elizabeth knew something was wrong the moment she entered Jessica's room. It couldn't be, but it was. The room was clean! Not a thing was out of place. There were no clothes lying around, and all the magazines were in neat piles on the dresser. It didn't look as though anyone lived there, and certainly not Jessica Wakefield.

Elizabeth thought whimsically that maybe the Environmental Protection Agency had finally forced her twin to clean up. In its usual state, the room certainly resembled a toxic-waste dump.

Elizabeth walked to the closet to put back the scarf she had borrowed. What she saw made sense of the clean room and everything else that had happened in the last few days, including Jessica's silence and her tears that morning. The closet was almost totally empty!

Elizabeth screamed at the top of her lungs. "Mom, Dad!" She ran down the stairs and out to the driveway. "Jess is gone." Elizabeth ran breathlessly to her father's side of the car.

"Of course," he said calmly. "She's at Lila's."

"No, I mean she's really gone!"

Her parents got out of the car and followed Elizabeth up to Jessica's room. They checked the closet and the drawers. Nearly everything had been cleaned out.

"Oh, my God," Alice Wakefield gasped.

"We'd better phone Lila," said Mr. Wakefield. "Maybe she knows something."

They went downstairs to the kitchen, and Elizabeth dialed Lila's number. While she was waiting for someone at the Fowler house to pick up the phone, Steven entered the room.

"What's up?" he asked.

His mother turned to him from her chair. Worry lined her youthful face. "We think Jessica's run away."

"Run away?" he said in disbelief. "What do you mean, run away?"

"Her clothes are all gone. Liz is calling Lila now."

The phone was picked up, and Elizabeth heard Lila's voice.

"Hello, Lila?" Elizabeth said.

"Yes? Oh, hi, Liz."

"Listen, Lila, is Jess there?"

Lila picked up the worried tone of Elizabeth's voice. "No. Why? Is something wrong?"

"When was the last time you talked to her?"

"Yesterday. She said she was going to be busy all weekend. What's up?"

Elizabeth decided against telling Lila what had happened. All they needed now was for something like this to get on the Sweet Valley gossip hotline.

"Nothing, Lila. I was just wondering where she

was, and I thought she might be over there." Elizabeth managed to conceal her mounting panic.

To her relief, Lila didn't pry. "Oh, well, she's not here. Listen, when she comes in, have her call me, OK?"

"Sure." Elizabeth thanked Lila and hung up. "Jess isn't there. Lila talked to her yesterday, but she hasn't seen her at all."

"OK. Everybody think," Mr. Wakefield said firmly. "Who might know something about all of this?"

"I think I've got an idea," Steven answered. "Liz, do you think she might be with Nicky?"

Elizabeth caught her brother's gaze. Of course! She should have thought of that herself.

"Who's this Nicky?" her father asked.

"Nicky Shepard," Elizabeth replied. "I think he lives over on Riverdale Drive."

Ned Wakefield reached for the phone book and a moment later began dialing the number.

After a second, he slammed down the receiver. "Damn! It's busy." He stood there for a moment looking grimly at the phone. "I'm going over there," he said, starting for the door.

Elizabeth followed him. "I'll go with you."

Her father moved with a determination Elizabeth had never seen before. "OK. You come with me. Steve, you stay here with your mother, in case Jess calls. Oh, and call Palomar House to tell Marianna we won't be making lunch.''

''Right.''

Elizabeth and her father walked quickly to the car and jumped in. She studied her father as they drove toward Nicky's house. He just kept his eyes on the road and remained silent.

Elizabeth thought about how Jessica had acted that morning. She could have kicked herself for not realizing how serious her twin had been. She should have done something when she saw Jessica in tears. Maybe if she had, none of this would have happened. Jessica would be home, and everything would be as it was.

She wanted to tell her father everything, all the things Jessica had said and done over the last few weeks that showed how much she resented her twin, and how impossible she felt her life at home had been. But this wasn't the time. All that was important now was finding her and bringing her home.

''This is it,'' Ned Wakefield said as he swung the car into the driveway of a low, ranch-style house.

He put the car in park and ran up to the front door, Elizabeth following close behind. Mr. Wakefield rang the door bell, and a small, frail-looking boy answered.

''Yes?''

"Hello. Is your mother or father home?" Mr. Wakefield asked.

"My mother is," the little boy replied. "But she's on the phone."

"Would you tell her there are some people here to see her, and that it's very important, please."

The little boy gave them a puzzled look and walked into the interior of the house. After a moment, a stern-looking woman in a pale-blue housedress came to the screen.

"Yes?"

"Mrs. Shepard? I'm Ned Wakefield. I believe my daughter Jessica has been seeing your son Nicky."

The woman looked at both of them suspiciously. "So?"

"Is Nicky home?" Elizabeth asked. "We'd like to speak to him."

"No, Nicky isn't home." The woman mimicked Elizabeth's tone. The mention of her son seemed to stir some hostility in her. "Although I would have expected *you* would have known that," she said pointedly to Elizabeth.

Elizabeth understood at once. "No—I'm not who you think I am. I mean there are two of us. You must mean my twin, Jessica."

"Oh, great," Mrs. Shepard said sarcastically. "Double trouble."

Ned Wakefield was losing his patience. "Look,

144

it's important that we talk to Nicky. Do you know where he is or when he'll be back?"

"Of course I know where he is," the woman snapped. "But I don't know when he'll be back. You'll just have to try again later."

She made a move as if to close the front door, but Mr. Wakefield sprang forward and grabbed it.

"Hey!" the woman shouted, taken aback.

"Look," Mr. Wakefield said tersely, "I'm not fooling around here. My daughter is gone, and I think your son might know something about it. Now where is he?"

The tone of his voice seemed to shake Nicky's mother up. She appeared to be on the edge of breaking down, and her voice took on a pleading tone. "Mr. Wakefield, I'm sorry. The truth is, Nicky's left home. We don't know where he's gone."

Ned Wakefield, too, appeared to be on the verge of tears. "Do you have any leads?"

"Well, we really haven't tried looking for him." Mrs. Shepard looked embarrassed. "See, Nicky's pretty headstrong, his father is very busy, and I've got my hands full with his brother Danny. He's not well, poor kid, and we have to watch him pretty close—"

"OK, Mrs. Shepard," he cut her off. "Thank you very much."

Mr. Wakefield turned quickly and went back to

the car. Elizabeth took a last look at Mrs. Shepard and followed him.

Mr. Wakefield said nothing as he started up the rust-brown LTD and backed it into the street. They were halfway home before he spoke.

"Why didn't we listen to her? How could she have gotten to this point without any of us seeing how serious it was?"

"I don't know, Dad. I just don't know." And for the first time in a long time, Elizabeth Wakefield felt absolutely helpless.

Steven and Mrs. Wakefield were still by the phone, where they had been when Elizabeth and her father left.

"Any word?" Mr. Wakefield asked his wife as they entered the kitchen.

Alice Wakefield shook her head mutely. Elizabeth knew her mother was a strong person, but at that moment she looked very pale and frightened.

"Did you talk to Nicky?" Steven asked them.

Elizabeth shook her head. "Nicky's taken off, too. His folks don't know where."

The four of them just looked at one another for a moment. Mr. Wakefield was the first one to say anything. He spoke in a quiet, confident tone. "OK. We are going to find her. First of all, we can be pretty sure that if we find Nicky we'll find Jess, right?"

Everyone nodded.

"OK," he went on, "so how do we find this Nicky? Any ideas?"

"His friends are all pretty different from our usual crowd," Elizabeth offered. "It might be hard to get them to cooperate."

"What do you mean?" her mother asked. "Why wouldn't they be willing to help?"

"You don't know this crowd," Elizabeth said.

Her father became angry. "What kind of people wouldn't understand a situation like this?"

Steven stood up. "Wait a minute. I think I know someone who might be able to help." He picked up the phone and began to dial.

Jessica decided she would just let the old lady sleep on her shoulder for a while. She looked around the bus station and frowned. The sunlight that streamed in from the big windows only made her feel worse. Everyone else in the place seemed to be happy, excited.

She tightened her grip on her suitcase handle and shifted her weight slightly to avoid waking the old lady again. The woman had taken the seat next to Jessica in the waiting room a full two hours earlier. After an hour of telling Jessica about her children and her good-for-nothing husband, she had fallen asleep on Jessica's shoulder. Whenever Jessica moved, the woman would wake up and hit her with her purse. Jessica could almost have laughed, if the experience hadn't been so unpleasant.

The man behind the ticket counter waved Jessica over. She managed to wriggle out from underneath the old woman without getting hit, and she made her way to the window.

"Listen, miss," the man said. "The last bus for San Francisco is leaving right now. You're going to have to take that one if you want to leave today."

Jessica looked around the station in panic. There was still no sign of her family. She had let three buses leave, but now she had to decide to go through with her plans or to give up.

"Thank you," she said to the man at the counter.

Jessica looked at the front door one more time, then walked toward the door to the buses.

She checked her watch. *The hearing must have been over hours ago, and they must have found my letter by now*, she thought. *So, Nicky was right. They really don't care about me. If they did, they would have been here by now, begging me to come home. Or maybe they thought I didn't have the guts to go through with it. Well, I'll show them!*

Defiantly, Jessica pushed her way through the double doors and headed for the bus, which was in the final stages of loading. She walked up to the driver and handed him her ticket.

"Is this the bus for San Francisco?"

He checked her ticket and nodded. "Yep. Just put your bags down over there and grab a seat. We'll be leaving in about five minutes."

Jessica sighed as she set her suitcases in the baggage area. She grabbed the handrail of the bus and pulled herself into it. Staring straight ahead of her, she walked to the back and settled in a seat by the window. Hoping for a last-minute reprieve, she looked at the people walking by the buses. A quick arrival by her mom, dad, Steven, and Elizabeth, a happy reunion, and she could go home, which was where she wanted to be more than she'd ever wanted anything.

Jessica was shaken from her thoughts by a familiar voice at her side. She looked around and saw the old woman from the waiting room taking the seat next to her.

"Well, if this isn't good luck, I don't know what is," the old woman cackled. "I hate taking this ride because I never have anyone to talk to, and now, here we are together, just like old friends. Won't this be fun?"

"Fun," Jessica said flatly. She sighed and tried not to cry as she stared out the window.

* * *

Steven talked excitedly as he waited for someone to answer the phone. "You remember Joe Seegar. He was on the basketball squad with me in high school. He's sort of in with Nicky's crowd, and he might be able to help." He paused as someone answered.

"Yeah?" the voice on the phone snapped.

"Joe, this is Steve Wakefield."

"Hey, hi ya, Steve. How's it going? What can I do for you?"

"Listen, I'm looking for Nicky Shepard."

"I know he took off, but I don't know where."

Steven sighed. His parents and Elizabeth stared at him hopefully from across the room. "That's too bad," he said casually to Joe Seegar. "I owe him a hundred bucks from last spring, and I finally got the money together. If you hear from him, tell him I want to pay him back."

Steven waited. Joe was silent on the other end of the phone for a moment. Then he said, "I know he needs the money right now, so I'll tell you. He's with Denny Wyatt, in San Francisco. You can probably get his number from information. The two of them got some kind of business thing going. Sorry I didn't tell you right off, Steve, but you never know. I always figure, if somebody wants somebody to know where they are . . . you know?"

"Sure," Steven replied. "Thanks a lot, Joe."

He hung up the phone and turned to his family. "Nicky's in San Francisco."

"San Francisco?" his father repeated. "You don't think Jessica would—"

Suddenly he sprang into action. "OK, the Fiat's still here, there are only two ways she could go, by bus or by plane. If she just left this afternoon, we may still be able to catch her."

"That's right," Alice Wakefield agreed. "Why don't you two take the bus station? Your father and I will take the airport."

"Right." Steven grabbed his car keys and headed for the door, Elizabeth following close behind.

"And listen." Their father halted them. "If you find her, make sure she knows we aren't mad at her. We just want her to come home."

Elizabeth fought back her tears. "I will, Dad. I will."

Thirteen

Steven turned his yellow Volkswagen into the parking lot and pulled into a space. He and Elizabeth unbuckled their seat belts and ran for the bus terminal.

There was a line at the ticket window, and Steven and Elizabeth stood at the end of it for a few moments. At the front of the line, a woman with two screaming children was quarreling with the ticket vendor over the price of a child's fare.

Steven kept glancing impatiently at the front of the line. Finally, he threw his hands up. "The hell with this stuff," he muttered as he pushed his way to the window.

"Hey!" the woman exclaimed.

"Excuse me," Steven said, "but this is an emergency."

He turned to the startled ticket agent. "Did you sell a ticket to a Jessica Wakefield today?"

"We don't take names on the tickets."

"Well, she's a young girl, about five feet six, very pretty with blue-green eyes and . . ." Steven sighed. "Wait a minute." He took hold of Elizabeth and pushed her toward the window. "She looks just like this."

The ticket agent looked at Elizabeth in surprise. "What happened, miss? I thought you were going to board that last bus."

Elizabeth and Steven exchanged glances. "A bus for San Francisco?" Steven demanded.

"Why, yes. What's going on here?"

"Has that bus left?" Elizabeth asked him.

"It's leaving just now," the agent replied. "Gate three."

Steven and Elizabeth pushed their way through the complaining crowd at the window and ran to the departure gate. They got there just as the bus pulled out.

Elizabeth ran after the bus, yelling for it to stop, but the driver didn't hear her.

"Oh, Steve!" Elizabeth exclaimed. "We missed her."

"Come on." Steven headed back toward the building. "We haven't lost yet."

Steven rushed into the station and pushed in front of the same woman, who was still arguing about the fare.

"Now, just a minute," she yelled.

"That bus," Steven demanded. "What's the next stop?"

"Look, buddy, you can't just push your way into line like that," the ticket agent responded.

"What's the next stop!" There was no mistaking Steven's urgent tone.

The agent backed off. "Carver City," he said.

"Thank you," Steven said. With Elizabeth in tow, he rushed out of the station.

The agent looked after them. "You're welcome."

Steven put the car into gear and headed north on the old highway.

"We'll never make it." Elizabeth moaned. "The bus has a good five-minute head start."

"We'll make it," Steven said. His voice was filled with determination, and his knuckles were almost white as he gripped the wheel and drove the car along the old country road at a high speed.

"What happens if we miss it, Steve?" Elizabeth asked desperately.

"Then we drive to the next stop, and we keep doing that until we catch up to her. I don't care if we have to follow her all the way to San Francisco."

Elizabeth glanced at the fuel gauge. It was approaching empty. There was enough gas to get to Carver City, but after that, they'd have to refuel. That would set them back more time.

"This is more my fault than anybody's," Steven muttered. "I've been so wrapped up in myself, I haven't taken the time to realize what was going on with Jess."

"It isn't just your fault, Steve."

"No, that's probably true. But still, I've been so horrible to Jess lately. I'll never forgive myself if something happens to her."

Elizabeth tried to make her voice sound as reassuring as possible. "Nothing is going to happen to her."

"I just keep asking myself how this could have happened," Steven continued. "How could this have gone so far without any of us noticing?"

"Look, I'm Jessica's twin. I'm the person who's closest to her in the whole world, but even I don't know what's going on in that mind of hers sometimes."

They drove in silence for a while. Elizabeth had driven through Carver City a couple of times. She recognized the outskirts of the town and knew they were getting close.

"Do you know where the bus terminal is?" she asked her brother.

"I've got an idea," Steven answered.

But the tone of his voice didn't sound certain. Elizabeth crossed her fingers and prayed that he would find it quickly. They had no time to waste. Any delay might spell disaster.